THE ROAD TO REDEMPTION

A YOUNG GIRL'S JOURNEY AND
HER QUEST FOR MEANING

Amanda Childress

THE ROAD TO REDEMPTION

A Young Girl's Journey and Her Quest for Meaning

Amanda Childress

Christian Publishing House

Cambridge, Ohio

CPH Since 2005

Christian Publishing House

Professional Conservative Christian
Publishing of the Good News!

THE ROAD TO REDEMPTION: A Young Girl's Journey and Her Quest for Meaning by Amanda Childress

ISBN-13: 978-1-949586-85-5

ISBN-10: 1-949586-85-5

Table of Contents

To Granny Barbara, Papaw Jim,

and Uncle Terry:

Though you may be gone,

your memory and influence

lives on within my heart.

CHAPTER ONE

Stella Mae Clark was born in the year 1959 to loving parents, Marsha and Nathaniel Clark. They had lived in the rural farming town of Elyer's Grove in Southern Georgia all their lives. They were high school sweethearts who fell in love during ninth grade after he saved her from getting nailed in the face by a football. Nathaniel was nineteen with sandy blonde hair and eyes of dark blue. His physique was muscular, and his chiseled face was lightly covered in scruff. Nathaniel had joined the Army after graduating and quickly rose up through the ranks. Specialist Nathaniel Clark was one of the best soldiers his commanding officer had ever seen. Upon returning from his first deployment, he married Marsha Dillon. Marsha's chestnut brown, doe eyes were constantly fixed on him. He loved the way her light skin always smelled like coconuts and the way that she would twirl her hair around on her finger when she was nervous. She had never met a man as kind and compassionate as he was. Nathaniel was selfless and made friends with any stranger he would pass on the street. She was timid, but Nathaniel knew how to make the desire to fade into the background disappear. When he proposed after being deployed for a year, she couldn't say yes fast enough.

A year after their marriage, Marsha gave birth to a perfect bundle of pink. "She's perfect," Marsha whispered as the nurse laid her on her chest. She could hardly contain the tears as her newborn daughter grabbed her pinky finger. Tiny blue eyes looked up at her with such innocence. She nuzzled her daughter to her chest, afraid to ever let go. Her heart melted, and she wished that she could freeze this moment for eternity.

"Thank you, Lord, for a beautiful baby girl. I give her to you and promise to raise her to love you as I do. She is your child, Father, fearfully and wonderfully made in your image. Thank you for blessing us". Nathaniel smiled as the tears silently slid down his cheek. His bride winced at his words, but her love for her daughter was all that was on her mind.

Nathaniel quickly fell head over heels in love with his daughter. He was constantly rocking her and telling her stories from the Bible. Every night, he would sing her to sleep with verses from "Amazing Grace" and "Victory in Jesus." As she grew older, he would take her with him to church while Marsha would pick up shifts at the dress shop any chance she could get. Marsha grew up in a family that never attended church while Nathaniel was born a pastor's son. He knew he wanted his children to grow up knowing the Word of God, and Marsha was not going to deprive him of that, even if she did not attend services regularly herself. She would attend service on Easter and Christmas, only to feel uncomfortable and counting down the minutes until she could leave.

One evening, when she was four years old, Stella Mae was playing in her room as she heard the muffled conversation taking place between her parents, followed by the sounds of her mother sobbing inconsolably. A few moments later they appeared hand-in-hand in her doorway and Nathaniel told her that they needed to talk. He cradled Stella Mae in his arms and held her so tightly it was as if he were trying to commit her image to memory. Marsha stood behind her husband, with a soft hand on his shoulder as he brushed a strand of wavy, blonde hair back from Stella Mae's face to reveal her sparkling blue eyes. Every time her father looked at her, there was this little light that would shine and cause her blue eyes to dance in admiration.

"I'm afraid daddy has some bad news," Nathaniel began as he looked down at the smiling, innocent face of his pride and joy," Daddy got a call today, and I am going to have to go away for a little while." Nathaniel did his best to conceal his tears, but his broken heart wouldn't allow it.

Stella Mae looked up in confusion at her father's face. "Where are you going, daddy," her sweet voice squeaked, "can't I come with you?" Nathaniel looked back at his wife who was fighting back the tears with everything that she had.

"Remember how we talked about daddy protecting people from the bad guys," he asked her kindly. Stella Mae nodded her head in affirmation. "Well, daddy has to go protect people from the bad guys. I am going to be gone for a little while. You and mommy are going to have to take care of each other. But, what does daddy always say," he asked Stella Mae.

"God is always with us and will never leave us," Stella Mae replied with a smile on her face while her mother stood blankly.

"That's right, Princess. God will be with me, and He will be with you. Remember Joshua 1:9? 'Have not I commanded thee? Be strong and of good courage; be not afraid, neither be thou dismayed: for the Lord thy God is with the withersoever thou goest,'" Nathaniel reminded her.

Stella Mae held onto her father as if he would float away. "Please, come back home, daddy," her tiny voice trembled as she held onto him as the tears silently slid down his cheek and her mother had to excuse herself from the room. Her echoing sob sounded down the hall and became muffled as she closed herself in their room, secretly wishing for the same thing as well.

Several months had passed since Nathaniel's deployment. It was nearing time for Thanksgiving, and Stella Mae constantly begged her mother to read her Bible stories, but her mother always told her she was busy with work and she would have to wait. Stella Mae would go to church with her friend that lived next-door and would come home excitedly telling her mother about what she learned, and it only fell on deaf ears. There was such light in her eyes that almost angered her mother, although she could never tell why. All she wanted was for her husband to come back home to her, for him to be safe. She was a better person when he was around, a better mother.

One afternoon Marsha took Stella Mae with her to buy material for a new dress as they had received news that it was possible her father would be coming home soon. Stella Mae always loved watching her mother make dresses at home. Her mother had always had such an eye for style. Bouncing up and down, Stella Mae held her mother's hand as they made their way back to their house Marsha was laughing at the silliness of her daughter, admiring the warmth that flowed from her. As they approached the path leading to the house, two men in military uniform waited to greet them. As they grew closer and closer, the two men removed their hats, and Marsha noticed a small, worn Bible in the hands of one of the men. Marsha stopped dead in her tracks, the basket of cloth dropped in slow motion to the ground as Marsha stood frozen. "No, no" she kept repeating as the tears began to flood her eyes.

The two gentlemen made an attempt to calm her. "Mrs. Clark," the older gentleman began, "I am sorry to inform you that your husband, Nathaniel Clark, has been killed in action...". Marsha began screaming and crying, pounding her fists into the gentleman's chest. She dropped to her knees as the gentlemen tried to console her, but it was no use. All the while, Stella Mae stood watching her mother, her face a blank stone.

The younger gentleman walked over to her and calmly asked her if she understood what was going on. She looked at him with sad eyes and replied, "yes, my daddy isn't coming home".

CHAPTER TWO

They laid Nathaniel to rest a few days before Thanksgiving, his body buried in the field behind the house where he so often ran and played with Stella Mae. The tall stalks felt like taunting ghosts to her now, as her father would never again chase her and tickle her as they fell to the ground in each other's arms. Nothing would ever be the same.

After the funeral service, Stella Mae hid herself in her room attempting to drown out the sobs from her mother's room. That evening, in particular, Stella Mae could hear the hushed cries from her mother's room and left her room to crawl into bed in an attempt to console her mother. "It's okay, mommy. Remember what daddy said when we die we go home to Jesus. He's safe now, mommy," Stella Mae sweetly half-whispered to her mother who was trembling with tears. Suddenly, Marsha sat up and turned to face her daughter, her face full of hot anger.

"Your father was taken from us. What are we supposed to do, Stella Mae? How are we going to live? I can't support us on just a seamstress's salary. We have bills to pay, and now we have to pay for your father's funeral. You really think your daddy is safe? What about our safety? You think if Jesus loved you that He would take away your daddy? Then you're a fool, Stella Mae," Marsha blurted out in a hot rage as she turned her back on her daughter.

Stella Mae had no response. She quietly crawled out of her mother's bed and slowly closed the door and went back to her room. As she made it to her bed, she knelt beside her bed as her father would do with her every night. "God," she painfully whispered, please take care of my daddy. I miss him, but I know he is with you. Please be with mommy, I know she is sad and angry right now. I just want her to be happy again. Please help her, Jesus. I love you. Amen".

That night, something changed within Stella Mae. Fear consumed her. She loved her mother and didn't want to anger her, but she also loved Jesus. She decided to focus on her mother and making her happy again. She didn't know how she would do it, but she would find a way to bring back the smile her daddy used to bring to her mama's face. She began drifting away from the life her father wanted for her.

But that was nothing compared to the pulling away from that life that was to come, and the heartbreaking terror that would accompany it.

CHAPTER THREE

It had been a year since Nathaniel died and things were nothing like they used to be. Marsha lived in a constant melancholic state. Every night Stella Mae could hear her quietly cry from her bedroom. She also took it upon herself to help her mother pick up the slack around the house. She would wash the laundry and clean the house and help her mother cook supper. At only five years old, she was the most grown-up member of her household. All she wished for was for her mother to smile again, to smile the smile that her father would cause with his wit and love. But, that smile would never be seen again.

One day in the spring, Stella Mae sat at the kitchen table peeling potatoes for dinner as her mother came in with a smile on her face. "Honey, I have some wonderful news," she sing-songed, "I met the most wonderful man today. We are going out to dinner tonight, so Mrs. Crawley is going to come sit with you". Marsha whirled her way down the hall to her room, leaving Stella Mae at the table in disbelief. It had only been a year since her father passed away and now her mother was moving onto another man. An uneasy feeling arose in Stella Mae's stomach, but she went back to peeling the potatoes and hiding how much she truly missed her father.

That evening, Mrs. Crawley came over and helped Stella Mae prepare a pot roast for supper. Suddenly, there was a knock at the door her mother so eagerly answered. She was dressed in a fancy dress with her hair pinned back in a barrette that belonged to her grandmother. Her mother's face was almost unrecognizable under the makeup, and she nearly suffocated her with the smell of her perfume. As she answered the door, a burly, gruff man stepped in the house. He smelled of cigarettes and whiskey. His full-grown beard made the deep brown of his eyes take on a possessed quality that frightened Stella Mae. She glanced down and noticed the cuts on his knuckles. He then turned to Marsha, "you ready?"

"Absolutely. Let's be on our way. Stella Mae, you be on your best behavior for Mrs. Crowley. Bye, dear," she sweetly replied as she kissed her frightened daughter on the forehead. She then turned on her heels and practically pranced out the door.

How could her mother like that man? He was rude and demanding, the complete opposite of her father. Where did she meet him? The local police station? She watched out the window as he helped her mother into his truck, and they drove away. A sinking feeling came over Stella Mae as a terrible thought came across her mind. A silent, fearful tear slid down her cheek as her mother disappeared over the hill.

What if this man became her mother's new husband, or worse, her new father?

CHAPTER FOUR

Marsha and William were married three months later, and within the first year, she gave birth to twin daughters, Virginia and Blanche. Stella Mae quickly faded into the background as her mother's new family began to take precedent. All her mother ever seemed concerned with was pleasing her drunk of a husband who came home every night smelling like an ashtray. Stella Mae was six now and would begin school in just a few weeks. She couldn't wait to be around children her own age and to have someone to talk to. She often found herself playing alone in the attic, which was now her room, filled with cobwebs and dust that often kept her awake at night through coughing fits. The sounds of the twins crying downstairs began to echo but could never conceal the angered screams from her stepfather. Marsha did her best to make him happy, but that seemed like an impossibility at this point. When he wasn't demanding her to silence the screaming infants, he was belittling her cooking or her appearance. Stella Mae couldn't help but notice her mommy had been wearing an awful lot of long-sleeved dresses and dark sunglasses. Her mother never said a word about it, but Stella Mae knew something wasn't quite right.

Stella Mae found herself unable to connect to her new stepfather. All he would ever do was yell at her and demand that she get out of his way. She learned that it was best to steer clear of her stepfather at any cost. She played with her dolls silently in her room and drew pictures of the way her family used to be. She kept the pictures concealed under her bed so her stepfather wouldn't find them and become angry with her, for she feared his punishment. She had a picture of her and her father that she kept in his Bible on her shelf. She would take it out every night and hold it to her chest as she would try to pray. It had been so long;

she couldn't really remember how. He was holding her in his arms in the field behind the house. That was one of her favorite memories and every day she clung to it to give her strength.

Finally, the day came when she would begin school. She woke early that morning to pack her paper bag lunch consisting of a turkey and cheese sandwich, an apple, and crackers. She stood in front of the mirror in a pink flower dress and tied a pink bow in her hair as she made herself look as presentable as she could. She quickly grabbed her notebook and ran down the steps. Marsha placed the twins in their car seats and drove her to school. Her mother walked her in and introduced her to her new teacher, Katherine Mayhew. Miss Mayhew was a young woman around twenty-two years old. She had dark chocolate hair and warm, green eyes that smiled along with her face. She stood outside her classroom and welcomed each child as they came in. Stella Mae gave her mother a hug and bounced into the room to find a seat. She found herself a desk and sat there taking in the classroom. Stella Mae pulled out her notebook and pencil and eagerly awaited instruction from Miss Mayhew.

"Mind if I sit here," a small voice chirped from beside her. Stella Mae turned to see a young girl about her age pointing to the desk next to hers. She had her black hair tied in pigtails with red ribbon and emerald eyes that shone like gemstones. Her cheeks were covered in freckles, and her smile lit up her entire face.

"I don't mind," Stella Mae replied as the young girl took her seat and unpacked her backpack. "I'm Stella Mae Clark. What's your name," she asked sweetly.

"I'm Carla Marie Yoast," the young girl replied, "It's nice to meet you, Stella Mae."

"It's nice to meet you too, Carla," Stella Mae answered back.

A few minutes had passed, and Miss Mayhew closed the door and made her way to the front of the classroom. "Good morning, class," she warmly chirped as the children echoed back. "I am very excited to meet all of you. I believe that we will have a wonderful year together". Miss Mayhew scanned the room and caught the glance of Stella Mae, offering her a smile. "I always like to start class off with a prayer. So, let's bow our heads, shall we". She began to pray, "Father, I ask that you be with these children, that they may grow to love learning. I pray that you be with me, Father, and give me the words to reach them. Be with us and keep us safe. In your precious and Holy name, I pray. Amen".

"Amen," Stella Mae whispered under her breath.

Lunchtime had finally come around and the children dispersed throughout the courtyard in their groups. Stella Mae took her bagged lunch under an oak tree and began to eat her sandwich. After a few minutes, Carla walked over to her and asked if she could join her, to which Stella Mae agreed.

Carla began to tell Stella Mae all about her parents, Barb and Oscar, and how her mother was a nurse at the hospital and her father was a merchant at the General Store in town. She was the youngest of six children, the only little girl of the mix. She also told Stella Mae about her Golden Retriever, Ashby, and how after church every Sunday they go down to the river and play with Ashby and fish off the bank.

"What about your family," Carla inquired as she bit into her Granny Smith apple and made a face at the sourness.

Stella Mae's face fell. "Well," she began, "my daddy died when I was younger. I can't remember him much now. My mommy got remarried to a new man. He really isn't all that nice. I do have two new little sisters, but they

19

cry a lot". Stella Mae took a big bite of her sandwich and continued, "my daddy used to teach me about the Bible and take me to church. But ever since he died, I don't get to go anymore".

"I'm sorry," Clara offered sweetly as the two finished their lunch.

"Thanks," Stella Mae replied quietly. The remainder of the lunch hour the two talked about dolls and dresses, never again mentioning what Stella Mae had told Clara about her life. All the while, Miss Mayhew stood at the steps to the school within earshot of the two little girls and heard the entire story.

"Lord," Miss Mayhew prayed silently," I lift little Stella Mae up to you. Be with her and her family, Father. Bring them back to You. If it be Your Will, Lord, give me the words to say to lead her back to You and to help her. In your precious name I pray. Amen".

CHAPTER FIVE

Over the next several months, Stella Mae began to truly flourish in her studies. She was reading better than some of the other children in the class and constantly had her nose in a book, whether she could read it yet or not. Miss Mayhew was astounded by the maturity she had seen in Stella Mae. She knew that sweet little girl had to come from a good family. She was one of the sweetest and kindest souls she had ever met. If someone forgot their lunch, Stella Mae was the first to offer them part of her healthy, homemade meal. If someone, even one of the boys that pick on Stella Mae didn't understand their arithmetic, Stella Mae would spend her recess helping them learn how to do their problems.

It came time for the annual Christmas play. Stella Mae had been assigned the role of Mary, and she took the role to heart. She stayed up, day and night, to learn each of her lines and to work on how exactly she wanted to deliver them. Joey Nelson was playing Joseph and, even though he smelled like pickles, Stella Mae used her little servant's heart to push on through. The anticipation for the night of the play was building. All of the children spent the morning of Christmas Eve at the church decorating and setting up the background. Miss Mayhew had never seen so many smiling faces or the children so dedicated. She was giddy with excitement.

The children's families filed in and took their seats. The play went off without a hitch. Every line was perfectly executed and the roar of applause at the end echoed off the walls. After the kids took their bows, they all went to find their families and enjoy refreshments. Amid the hustle and bustle, Miss Mayhew looked outside to see Stella Mae sitting on the steps of the church alone. She walked over to her and placed her hand gently on her back as she took a seat beside her. "You did a great job," Miss Mayhew smiled. "I am sure that you will do just as great next year." She was so caught up in the excitement of the play's success, she didn't notice the tears silently sliding down Stella Mae's cheeks until she looked up at her, her eyes blue against a reddened background.

Stella Mae just hung her head. "Maybe, but mommy still won't come," she painfully replied as she got up and slumped her way down the path, leaving Miss Mayhew to her own tears.

_____

About a week later, Miss Mayhew noticed she hadn't seen Stella Mae since the night of the play. She decided to pay her family a visit to make sure that she was okay. As she stood outside knocking on the door, she could hear screaming and crying from inside. Stella Mae appeared at the door with a crying baby on her hip. As she opened the door, Miss Mayhew could see another baby lying in a bassinet.

"Hi, Miss Mayhew. What are you doing here," Stella Mae asked as she tried to hush her screaming sister on her hip and bounced her up and down.

"I- I've missed you at school this week," Miss Mayhew spoke with worry in her voice, "I just wanted to come by and make sure you're okay. Is your mommy home"?

Stella Mae quickly left from the doorway to grab a pacifier and set her sister down on the blanket in the living room. She walked back over to Miss Mayhew as she picked up some clothing along the way. "Mommy and William aren't here. They had to go out of town. I needed to stay here to take care of the babies," she replied.

"Oh," Miss Mayhew answered in surprise, "well, who is staying with you"?

"Nobody. Mrs. Crawley comes over every now and then to check on us, but she's older, so it's hard for her to get over here. Mommy told me to stay here and that they would be back in a couple of weeks. She said that I didn't need to go to school anymore because she needs my help with the twins," Stella Mae sadly informed Miss Mayhew. "I'm sorry, Miss Mayhew. I loved coming to school every day."

Miss Mayhew couldn't believe what she was hearing. This little girl was barely seven years old, and her mother was forcing her to stay home and care for two babies that had to barely be nine months old. She looked at the counter and noticed the fixings of pot roast and that the start of a dress laid on a chair in the living room. It was then that she began to realize that all the while Stella Mae had been supporting herself. She had been cooking all of those home cooked meals, and she had been the one sewing all the beautiful dresses she wore. Her heart began to break.

Suddenly, a burly man appeared in the doorway with a woman who looked like she was frightened for her life. "Who the devil are you," his deep voice growled as anger flashed in his eyes. "What are you doing in my house"?

"My, my name is Katherine Mayhew. I am Stella Mae's teacher. I noticed she hadn't been at school in a while and I just wanted to make sure everything was okay," she shakily replied.

"She won't be comin' back to school. She's needed here. Now, I'd very much appreciate it if you'd get out of my house," William grumbled.

"Well, I-I would be happy to come by in the evenings and help Stella Mae with her studies. She is a very bright young girl, and I would hate to see-".

"I said, get out," William slurred as he grabbed Miss Mayhew's arm and practically dragged her out the front door.

She looked back and saw the broken look on Stella Mae's face just as the door was slammed in her face, and her own tears began to cascade down her cheeks.

CHAPTER SIX

By the time Stella Mae had turned sixteen, she was taking care of her twin sisters, two little brothers, and another little baby sister. In a family of eight, Stella Mae had never felt more alone. What she *felt*, was used. It wasn't her mother or stepfather who would get up with a screaming baby at 2:00 AM. It wasn't her mother who stayed up for 48 hours when three of her siblings came down with the flu. It wasn't her mother who made sure the kids were fed, bathed, and rocked to sleep each night, it was Stella Mae.

She couldn't even remember the last time she had been to church or even touched her daddy's Bible, which she used to read every chance she had just to feel close to him. Honestly, Stella Mae felt abandoned, by everyone. Her father died, her mother threw her away, and God forgot her. She felt nothing any longer. A feeling of emptiness overtook her.

As she was in the market one Saturday afternoon, she ran into a familiar face from her younger days, Henry Oliver. She had had a crush on him for years. Henry Oliver was a couple of years older than Stella Mae, by now he had to be eighteen. She did her best to avoid eye contact, but she couldn't help but get lost in Henry's brown eyes. She loved the way his hair was always slicked back, like someone in a greaser movie.

She couldn't help but notice that Henry grew up very well. Working with his dad in the hayfields did wonders for his muscles. He had to be at least 6' 9" since she last saw him, when he was fourteen years old, and she was just a young ten-year-old infatuated, lovesick little girl.

"Well, if it isn't little Stella Mae," his deep voice called from across the way. Surely, he couldn't be talking to her, in her simple, tattered dress she had to teach herself to sew that was being practically ripped off her by the two little boys hanging from her legs. There is no way someone like him would ever talk to her. "What," he teased," don't remember your name"?

Stella Mae could feel the blood rushing to her face. She had always dreamed of this moment but never expected that it would ever actually come true. She tried her best to seem as composed as she could as she smoothed her dress and did the best to ignore the two little boys on the edge of ripping her dress. "Oh, hey Henry," she replied sheepishly.

"Look who finally grew up boys," he joked to his buddies that were with him. "I figured you were still about yea high." Stella Mae could feel the blood rushing back to her cheeks again. Why was he talking to her, of all people? He was smart, strong, and handsome. He could have his pick of any girl in the town, and here he was talking to her. "Listen," he began, "a couple of us are going down to Houston's Creek tonight. You should come". Stella Mae's heart began to race. She was finally being invited to be a part of something. She knew that her mother would never let her go. She would have to stay there and take care of the kids because heaven forbid, she should take care of her own kids and not spend every waking minute trying to win the approval of her new husband.

Still, she wanted to go with Henry. Hadn't she earned it? She did all of the cooking and the cleaning and taking care of her siblings. What does her mom do? She sits around all day fawning over her husband and drinking so much her liver had to be drowning. Her step-father came home drunk about every evening and would pass out in his chair. Some nights she would hear them arguing, over the cries of the babies screaming, and then she would hear loud thuds followed by her mother sobbing. What was Stella Mae to do? She was a hundred pounds soaking wet, and her stepfather was about 280 pounds. There was no way she could go up against him. Then again, she thought to herself, why should she? Her mother practically abandoned her, why should she help her when she has done nothing for her?

She thought about her mom and her life up until this point. The next thing she knew, she was saying she would love to meet them there. "Great," Henry's blue eyes danced as he smiled, "see you tonight." Stella Mae watched him walk away as a gnawing feeling threatened to eat its way out of her stomach.

What had she gotten herself into?

CHAPTER SEVEN

Stella Mae finally got the last baby to sleep and began fixing herself up to meet Henry. She wore a pink dress, which she had sewn herself, that was trimmed with lace around the collar and the hem. She pulled her blonde curls back with a hair barrette she snuck from her mother's room and highlighted her cheeks with a little blush. She stood back and stared into the mirror as she smoothed down the dress. This gnawing feeling started in her stomach as her heart raced a million miles a minute. Her eyes went to the picture of her and her father when she was a baby. He was dressed in his army uniform and holding her in the air. Her face was radiant and consumed by her smile. She missed her father with her whole heart. She would give anything to have him back, to just leave with him and go away. In a way, when she lost her father, she lost her mother too.

She grabbed her sweater and slowly opened her door to make sure the coast was clear before sneaking out the front door. She walked about four miles down to Houston's Creek and could see Henry standing by the fire. Even in the firelight, he made her heart skip a beat. She stood for a minute watching him as she took a deep breath. Slowly, she made her way over to where he was standing with his friends. He smiled as she gave him a slight wave.

"Hey, she made it," he smiled as he took a drink from a brown paper bag before passing it off to one of his friends. He walked over and put his arm around her shoulder. She knew the smell of whiskey immediately that was emanating from his lips, which made her feel uneasy. It reminded her of her stepfather, and his image flashed through her mind. "You hungry? We have some burgers over here if you want one," he offered.

28

"No, thank you," she replied quietly. She looked around and noticed several of his friends with their faces practically plastered to the faces of several girls. A shudder traveled down her spine. Henry walked over to the edge of the creek and sat down on a large rock, patting the space next to him. Stella Mae slowly sat down next to him, her palms dripping with sweat. "This is my favorite spot. My dad started bringing me here when I was four. We'd go fishing every weekend and go hunting in those woods," he smiled as he pointed to the land across the way. She was dazzled by the smile across her face. She forgot that people were actually capable of having a good relationship with their parents. As far as she was concerned, she was nothing but an orphan.

They sat there talking for hours about their dreams and aspirations. He told her about how he wanted to open a homemade furniture store, and she told him about how she wanted to travel the world. She wanted to do something that mattered. She had spent most of her life reading books about adventures and about these incredible stories, but the story of her life was nothing but a blank page. "My dad used to tell me about all of these different places that he used to go to," she started telling him as they sat with their feet in the water. "I want to go see the world. I want to go anywhere but here. Dad always made it seem like there was this whole other existence out there. Anywhere is better than here."

"What do you mean? I thought you loved living here," he asked inquisitively.

She picked a flower and threw it into the creek. "I just, I need a change of scenery and a change of pace. I don't want to be cramped up here forever taking care of my siblings. My mom treats me like I'm just a servant, not even part of the family. My stepfather abuses her, but she's too scared to leave him. There's nothing I can do about it. I'm just sick of it all. I want to go out and see what else the world has to offer," she replied with desperation in her voice. They continued to talk for hours and, somewhere between all of the talking and all of the laughter, he had convinced her to try some of the paper covered bottle. She was reluctant, but she had been having so much fun with him, she didn't want to seem like a child.

It burned the whole way down and made her stomach queasy. They continued drinking and laughing and talking well into the evening. All of his friends and their ladies had long gone home. Stella Mae and Henry laid back on a blanket and just stared at the stars. Her head was spinning, but she had never felt happier than at that moment with Henry as she laid her head on his chest. All of that happiness faded the following morning as the bright sun woke her up, along with a pounding headache.

It wasn't until the moment she finally adjusted her eyes and sat up to see a pile of clothes around them that the happiness she once felt immediately turned to shame and regret.

She had managed to get home before her mother and William ever woke up. She checked on her little siblings, who thankfully were all still fast asleep. She went into the powder room and tried to clean herself up. How could she have been so stupid? To allow herself to drink the very stuff she loathed that her stepfather drank every single day and then to allow *that* to happen. How could she have been so reckless?

She threw some water in her face and stared into the mirror. It was like looking into her father's eyes, his disappointment reflecting back. A shiver traveled down her spine as her nails dug into the basin. She collapsed to the floor in convulsing tears. Her wet hair clung to her face. She sat there on the ground pounding her fists into the floor until her knuckles started to turn red.

The cries of her youngest sister snapped her back. She pulled herself up, used a towel to wipe her face, and went into the nursery. She picked up the tiny bundle of pink and held her tight to her chest. She sat down in the rocking chair as she hummed to and hushed her sister. After she calmed down, Stella Mae lay her sister where she was facing her. She looked into her innocent brown eyes, and again the tears escaped from her eyes. "What have I done," she whispered to the tiny bundle. Her sister only replied with a gentle coo.

As Stella Mae sat rocking her innocent little sister, she couldn't help but think about what her life had been like the past couple of years. Then, the events of last night came flooding back to her, making her nauseous and trembling. Little did she know that that one night would completely change the course of her life.

Forever.

CHAPTER EIGHT

A few weeks had passed since that night. Stella Mae hadn't heard from or seen Henry since she had left that morning. She threw herself into caring for her siblings and the house in an effort to distract herself from all she had been feeling. She thought for sure she must be overdoing things a little. She was finding herself feeling exhausted and had decided she had caught some kind of stomach bug. She had gotten sick several times and was constantly nauseous.

Finally, one day came when her mother and William were going to take the children to visit William's parents in Savannah. Of course, Stella Mae was left at home, but she didn't seem to mind. It was peaceful to have the house to herself and to not have to worry about making bottles or changing diapers. She would miss her siblings, but if she was being honest with herself, they were the only ones she would miss.

She waved goodbye to them from the doorway and watched as they disappeared down the dirt road. She closed the door and decided to go into town to buy supplies she would need while her family was away. She started browsing through the market when she heard a familiar voice behind her. "Stella Mae? Stella Mae Clark? Is that you?"

She turned around and came face to face with Miss Mayhew. "Miss Mayhew? Hi, how-how are you," Stella Mae asked in a nervous tone.

"I'm doing great. Still teaching, just at a different school. I actually got married a couple of years ago, and we had a beautiful baby boy," Miss Mayhew chirped. "My husband, Adam Elliston, owns a farm just a little way past the school. What have you been up to? I've missed seeing you. I wanted to reach out but…", she trailed off, obviously thinking about her last encounter with William.

Tears started to well up in Stella Mae's eyes as her hands started to tremble. Mrs. Elliston took her in her arms and held her as she broke down in sobs. Stella Mae couldn't control herself long enough to speak. She finally agreed to go to Mrs. Elliston's farm for a cup of tea. The entire drive there Stella Mae's hands were trembling as she twirled them in her lap.

Mrs. Elliston opened her door and set her basket down on the table as she went over to the fire to begin filling the tea kettle. Stella Mae took a seat at the small table and took note of the house as she sat picking the skin of her nails. The house felt so warm and inviting, just the way that she used to feel when she was still able to go to school. There were flowers everywhere and the sun made the room bright and open. Mrs. Elliston came and sat down beside her, slowly taking Stella Mae's hand in hers. Her eyes were, just as they had always been, so kind. When she talked to someone, it was like she was looking into that person's soul, trying so deeply to connect and understand that person. She was the one person Stella Mae ever truly felt safe around, aside from her father.

Stella Mae took a deep, ragged breath as she wiped the tears from her cheek with her other hand. She told Mrs. Elliston everything. She told her about how her stepfather was abusing her mother, how he was a raging alcoholic, how she was forced to take care of her siblings because her mother and stepfather only saw her as a servant. Then, she broke down in uncontrollable sobs as she told her about that night down by the river. Right about that time, the scream of the tea kettle nearly sent Stella Mae into the ceiling.

Mrs. Elliston quickly rose from her seat and removed the kettle from the fire. She took her seat again and wiped the hot tears from Stella Mae's cheeks. "Stella Mae, what happened does not make you a bad person. Don't ever let anyone talk you into thinking otherwise. You are one of the sweetest young women I know. That night does not make you anything less than that," Mrs. Elliston spoke warmly.

In between sobs Stella Mae managed to choke out the words, "I can't help it. I've been sick for weeks, and my body is physically worn down. My stomach aches all the time. I can't sleep at night because I just keep replaying that night over and over in my head. I just can't help but think about how disappointed my father would be if he were still alive. How could I have been so stupid?"

As she spoke, the expression on Mrs. Elliston's face changed. She took a deep breath and took both of Stella Mae's hands in hers. "First of all," she began, "you can call me Katherine. Second of all, Stella Mae, I don't really know how to tell you this. Stella Mae, honey, I think you're pregnant."

CHAPTER NINE

Stella Mae sat there motionless and silent. The world around her fell into a silence she had never experienced. The only sound that could be heard was the sound of her heart demanding its escape from her chest. Those four little words from Katherine were playing over and over, like a broken record of the world's worst song. The room began to spin, and it immediately felt like flames were engulfing her.

She came back to reality as Katherine took a cold washcloth and patted it gently on her face. "Stella Mae are you okay, sweetie," she asked warmly.

She didn't know how to answer that question. She was only sixteen. What was she supposed to do? There was absolutely no way she could go home and tell them she was pregnant. She feared what William would do to her if he found out. She had nowhere else to go. Her mother would offer her no help if she found out. She had no other family, nowhere to take refuge. She knew how to care for children since she practically raised her siblings. But a child of her own? She wasn't ready for that. What about Henry? A sinking feeling in her stomach began to take over. Should she tell him? What would he say? How would he react? Would he want her to keep the baby or would he do away with her altogether?

"Breathe. Stella Mae, breathe," Katherine's calm voice was trying to reassure her as she continued dabbing her face with the cool cloth.

Stella Mae released a ragged breath. "I, I can't do this," she finally managed to utter as she desperately tried to catch her breath. "I'm only sixteen. I never even finished school. How am I supposed to take care of a child? I have no money, no job, no education. And what about Henry?

What is he going to think?" She was in hysterics by this point. She was pacing back and forth in the living room so fast. Katherine was sure she was going to wear a hole into the floor.

Katherine got up and walked over to her and wrapped her in her arms. She assured her that everything was going to be okay. She herself let out an exasperated sigh. "I have an idea, but you may not like it," she began. "My mother has a house in the next town over, Sawyer Mills. My father passed away several years ago, and my mom is just living there by herself. Stella Mae," she whispered as she took her hands and lightly cupped Stella Mae's face, "do you want to take care of this baby?"

Stella Mae's head hadn't stopped spinning. She kept thinking of her father, of her innocent siblings that would likely suffer with her gone. She even thought of her mother and how no one would be there to protect her from William if she left. Then, almost as if involuntary, her hand went to her stomach. She closed her eyes as hard as she could. She took in a deep breath and released with her whole body. With all she could muster she choked out one tiny word that surprised her and would change her life forever.

"Yes".

She made the decision to find Henry and tell him the news. Her entire body trembled in fear. How would he react? Would he be happy? Would he be angry? It was like a reel was playing over and over in her head of the best and worst scenarios. She constantly went back and forth with her decision to tell him, but ultimately, she felt it was the right thing to tell him he was going to be a father.

She made it to his front door and took a breath so deep it must have come from her feet. She knocked on the door and held her breath until the moment he opened the door. "Stella Mae," his deep voice greeted her, "what are you doin' here"?

She could fill a lake with the sweat dripping from her palms. In the middle of summer, it felt like it was ten thousand degrees. "We need to talk," she shakily replied. He closed the door behind him and led her over to a bench under one of the Oak trees in his front yard. She looked at him and tried her hardest to remember what it was that drew her to him. Was it just his looks or was it about wanting the unattainable? There was nothing special about her. She wasn't beautiful like some of the other girls her age. She didn't fawn over the boys or try to make herself seem helpless, so one of them would come to her rescue. She was simple. She taught herself to cook and how to sew. She loved reading to her siblings and staying up at night with a flashlight to read book after book. Now that she had this new life growing inside of her, she wondered what she ever saw in Henry.

"What did you want to talk about," Henry asked with a hint of nervousness in his voice. He stuck his hands down in his pocket as he leaned against one of the oak trees in his yard.

Stella Mae began picking the skin of her nails as her leg bounced nervously. She took a deep breath and released it with a heavy sigh. "I- I have something that I need to tell you. Do you remember that night down at the river?" Henry sighed and rubbed his hand on the back of his neck, almost like he seemed embarrassed of that night. He replied that he remembered. "Look, I- I don't really...I don't know how to..." she tried to sputter.

"Spit it out, Stella Mae. You're makin' me more nervous than a cat in a room full of rockin' chairs," he half-joked.

"I'm pregnant," she finally blurted. Henry's face went white and turned to stone. For a minute, she was worried he was going to fall over. She repeated his name multiple times to try to get his attention, to get him to at least acknowledge that he heard what she had said. He immediately got up and started pacing as he rubbed his hands over his head.

"No. No. No," he panicked, "You can't be serious. I'm eighteen, Stella Mae. I haven't even gone to college yet. I ain't ready to be a dad. My parents are going to kill me. You can't be serious." He started pacing back and forth in the yard with his hands on his head as he spoke. His face turned as red as the tomatoes his mom grew in their garden.

"I'm serious, Henry. I am having a baby, your baby. Look, I didn't plan for this to happen, but it did. We can't take that night back. But look, we have a choice to make. I'm leaving. I am getting out of here to prepare a life for this child to grow up in. You can come with me. Look, I'm only sixteen. I'm scared too. I can't do this by myself. Henry I..." Stella Mae pleaded.

"Look, you're a nice girl and all Stella Mae. I just... don't... like you like that. I'm not ready to settle down and start a family. Look at me, I can't raise a kid. I've got plans," his words fell harsh on Stella Mae's ears.

Stella Mae instinctively put her hand to her stomach. "Okay," she whispered softly, "I understand. Take care of yourself, Henry. Maybe I'll see you again some day. But I need you to hear me. This choice you're making right now, it's permanent. If you walk away from this child now, you walk away forever. There is no changing your mind down the road. Do you understand that Henry", she shakily replied as the tears began to brim her eyes.

All Henry could do is drop his head as he sighed. Then, he looked up at her with wet eyes, "Goodbye, Stella Mae."

CHAPTER TEN

Thankfully, Stella Mae's family wouldn't be back until the end of the week. Katherine went with her to pack up her belongings before taking her to her mother's house. Stella Mae opened the door to her dusty attic. She grabbed a suitcase and stuffed all she could into it. As she packed, she came across her father's old Bible and found her favorite picture in the front. Thoughts of what her father would think flooded her mind, but she quickly shook those thoughts away as she stuffed the Bible into the suitcase.

She walked one last time into her siblings' room. She took the blankets she had made for each of them in her hands as she ran her fingers over the names she stitched with love. She could feel the tears coming again, but she immediately wiped them away and placed everything back in its place. She thought of her mother and how she hadn't always been cruel. Before her father died, she was a totally different person. She was full of life and happiness. Now, she was miserable and lived in fear.

She sat down in the parlor and decided to write her mother a goodbye letter. She hadn't expected to cry, but her tears stained the paper, leaving behind circular stains of heartache. She finally finished and read the letter to herself: *Dear mom, I'm sorry that I could not tell you goodbye to your face, but I was scared what would happen if William found out I wanted to leave. I love you, mom, and I love my brothers and sisters with all of my heart. I am sorry that it has come to this. I can't keep this secret from you anymore. I'm pregnant, mom. I know you won't understand. I made some bad choices, but now I have to do what is right for my baby and me. I hope that you will understand. You stopped seeing me as your daughter long ago. I would have given anything for a hug from you or for you to just see me as more than someone to watch after your other children. I'm sorry that things have to be this way. I pray you find peace and that you may truly see the life you are living. Please, take care of those kids. Get them out of there before he kills you or before he kills one of them. That is my greatest fear. Don't throw them away like you did me. Goodbye, mom! I love you. Truly yours, Stella Mae.*

She hid the letter in the pockets of one of her mother's coats, in the hopes that William would never find it. She followed Katherine out the door and turned around for one last look at the home she was leaving behind. "I have one last thing I have to do," she spoke softly. Katherine told her to take as much time as she needed, and she would be there when she was ready.

She went up the hill to where her father was buried. She dropped to her knees and pulled away the stalks of wheat that had grown around his tombstone. "Daddy," she whispered as a single tear hit the stone, "I'm so sorry. I know I've let you down. I've let myself down. I promise I will turn everything around. I promise. I love you, daddy. Please, forgive me." She gently kissed her fingertips and touched them lightly to his grave.

As she turned to leave, Stella Mae didn't yet understand all that she had left behind that day and how it would take nearly losing everything she had before she could ever begin to find it again.

They had arrived that evening at the home of Katherine's mother, Mrs. Abigail Mayhew. Mrs. Mayhew was every bit of five feet tall with her grey hair tied up in a braided knot. She reminded Stella Mae so much of Katherine. As soon as she met Stella Mae, she wrapped her arms around her as if she had known her entire life.

She took her by the hand and let her to the room she had set up for her. It wasn't anything fancy. The bed had been turned down and was covered by a quilt that had obviously been stitched by Mrs. Mayhew. A small bookcase sat in the corner with a couple of books on the shelves. What really got to Stella Mae was the small wooden crib that sat beside the bed. She walked over to it and ran her hands along the carved wood. It was painted white with pink flowers hand painted on the side. Katherine Joy Mayhew was painted in lilac cursive at the foot of the crib. "My Charles painted that when we found out, we were expecting Katherine," Mrs. Mayhew reminisced.

She could do this, right? She could raise a baby and be a good mother. She had had enough practice with her siblings and taking care of the house. Her hand immediately went to her stomach. She didn't have much of a choice. She was all this precious blessing had. She made a promise to herself that she would give this baby the life she never had. This baby would never feel unloved, unwanted, or unworthy. She would be the mother she wishes she had growing up, at least once her father passed away.

"I'll leave you to unpack your things. Just come into the kitchen when you're done. I'll put on some tea," Mrs. Mayhew spoke warmly as she gave Stella Mae's shoulder a gentle squeeze and then closed the door.

Stella Mae sat down on the bed and opened her suitcase. She pulled out her father's Bible and caressed the worn edges. She got down on her knees, facing the bed, and pulled out the picture of her and her father. Then, Stella Mae did something that she hadn't done since she was a young girl. "Dear God, I need your help. I cannot do this on my own. I know I have Katherine and her mother, but I need you, Lord. I need your strength and guidance. I'm scared, Lord. Please, help me to love and support this child. Forgive me of my sins, Father. Help me to seek you. And, Lord, be with my siblings. Protect them and watch over them. And," she began to let the tears slide down her cheeks as her hands trembled, "be with my mother. Keep her safe, Lord. She needs you. Those precious babies need you. Tell Daddy I'm sorry, Father." She began to fully break down into heaving sobs. "Tell him I'm sorry I left you, Lord. Tell him I'm sorry I ended up here and that I couldn't save my mom. Tell him, tell him I love him, God. In the precious name of Jesus, I pray. Amen"

She sat in the floor for several minutes more, clutching her father's picture to her heaving chest repeating over and over how sorry she was. Finally, she caught her breath, kissed her father's picture and placed it back in the front of the Bible. She wiped the tears from her face and smoothed her dress.

Would this be what leads her back to the arms of her Heavenly Father, or would this only be the first of many stumbling blocks that would completely break her? She slowly turned the door knob, let out a deep exhale, and joined the two women, who had saved her life, for tea.

CHAPTER ELEVEN

Katherine remained with them for a few days to help get Stella Mae settled. She went with her to meet the doctor in town, Clayton Morris, an older gentleman with a scruffy white beard who had been the Mayhew family doctor since Katherine was born. He assured Stella Mae that he would be with her every step of the way and that she could always come to him with any questions or concerns. The night before she left, Stella Mae prepared a home cooked meal for Katherine and her mother as a way to say thank you for their hospitality and help. She refused to let them lift a finger and sent them into the living room while she cleared the table.

Once Mrs. Mayhew went to sleep, Katherine and Stella Mae remained in the living room as they sipped tea. As Katherine was taking a slow sip Stella Mae quietly whispered, "I can't tell you how much all of this has meant to me. I haven't really had anyone care about what happens to me since my dad died. I had kind of forgotten what a family could feel like."

Tears silently forced their way out of Katherine's eyes as she took Stella Mae's hand in hers. "Sweetie, you always have a family here. I know that things right now are scary, but I know your heart. You are going to be a great mother. You have me and my mother by your side. Always. I promise you that. God is going to do great things with you, Stella Mae. I knew that from the moment that you walked into my classroom as a bright-eyed little girl."

Stella Mae felt something flutter within her. She had always heard her father say that God had a plan and a purpose for her life as a child. She could remember the preacher always saying that God loves us no matter what. He wants us to accept Him and to love Him with our whole hearts. Stella Mae wondered if God still loved her, after what she had done. Did He still remember her even though she hadn't really spoken to Him since she was a child up until a couple of days ago? She felt something missing in her life, but she felt for sure it was her father. She needed someone who cared for her.

Stella Mae simply thanked Katherine for her kind words. Katherine then asked if she could pray with Stella Mae, to which she reluctantly agreed. Katherine sat down both of their tea cups and took Stella Mae's hands in hers as she bowed her head. "Dear Heavenly Father, I just want to thank you for your goodness and mercy that you shower us with every day. I thank you that you are a God who loves and is just to forgive us of our sins. Father, I pray that you be with Stella Mae. Help her to raise this child to the best of her ability and give her strength. Father watch over her and help her to know that her strength comes from you. I ask you these things in your precious and Holy name. Amen." Then she took Stella Mae's face in her hands and whispered, "you're going to be okay." She wrapped her in the tightest and warmest hug she could manage.

For the first time in her life, Stella Mae finally believed that maybe, just maybe she was right. Everything really will be okay. Maybe she had finally found a piece of what she had been missing. A home.

_____

Over the next couple of months, Stella Mae worked alongside Mrs. Mayhew with her sewing business. At night, Mrs. Mayhew would help teach Stella Mae simple arithmetic and writing skills since she was a retired school teacher. While she would sit at the kitchen table working on problems and reading assignments, Mrs. Mayhew would sit on the couch and read her Bible. She would wake up early Sunday mornings to go to church, leaving Stella Mae in bed. Stella Mae couldn't understand why

Mrs. Mayhew never invited her to attend services with her. Six months she had been with her, and she never asked her once to go with her. Was she ashamed of her and her condition? Was she ashamed of her sin?

One night Stella Mae sat pushing around her carrots on her plate when she finally worked up enough courage to bring up church. "Mrs. Mayhew," she asked sheepishly as Mrs. Mayhew was elbow deep in dishwater, "I've been here for six months now. Why have you never invited me to go with you to church?"

Immediately, Mrs. Mayhew froze. It was only a couple of seconds, but to Stella Mae, it felt like an eternity. Slowly, she pulled her hands from the water and dried them on the towel on the counter. She quietly and slowly made her way over to the table where she sat across from Stella Mae as she took her hand. Her wrinkled hands felt small and soft, comforting to Stella Mae, but also terrifying. Her blue eyes glimmered as she looked so deep into Stella Mae's eyes she may as well have been looking into her soul. "Sweetie," she began quietly," I learned long ago that you can't force people to go to church. That's a choice you need to make on your own. I can't make it for you. I haven't asked you because I don't want you to feel like you have to go 'cause I asked you. I want you to go because *you* want to go. Because *you* want to hear God's Word. Because *you* feel led to go."

Mrs. Mayhew stood up and walked back over to the sink where she went back to work on the dishes. Stella Mae sat there letting those phrases play over and over in her mind. Her stomach felt like it was going to explode. Her throat made it hard to breathe as her pulse quickened with every beat of her heart. She silently slipped away from the table and went into her room. She came back out holding something tight to her chest. As she appeared in the doorway, Mrs. Mayhew turned around to meet her gaze. She noticed the faded black Bible in her hands.

Stella Mae's voice shook, "Can I go with you to church on Sunday?"

No smile in the world could compare to the one that took over Mrs. Mayhew's face as she heard Stella Mae's words. She made her way over to her and put both of her hands on her arms as she whispered, "of course you can." She wrapped her in an embrace that silenced the beast in her stomach, and she couldn't help but smile too.

CHAPTER TWELVE

Sunday morning had finally come around, and Stella Mae made sure she was up early and ready. She cooked breakfast for Mrs. Mayhew of scrambled eggs, bacon, and fresh cut fruit. She wanted to find some way to thank her for allowing her to go to church with her and for all that she had done for her over the last six months. Mrs. Mayhew's face lit up as she walked into the kitchen and saw the meal before her. She thanked Stella Mae, and they sat down together and enjoyed breakfast as they laughed and talked.

The church was in the main part of town. It was nothing fancy, but something about it took Stella Mae's breath away. The outside of the building was made of beautiful cobblestones of pale grey. The pews were dark brown with red velvet cushion, and the pulpit had an intricate cross etched into the podium.

Multitudes of people came flooding over to where they were sitting to welcome them. It was apparent Mrs. Mayhew was a prominent member of the church the way that everyone respected her. Stella Mae could feel the warmth of their welcome washing over her. Eventually, everyone took their seats as the pastor made his way up to the podium. Reverend Isaiah Bower was an older gentleman, probably around 60 years old. What little hair he had was white and matched the neatly trimmed beard that covered his face. He instructed everyone to stand and sing the first three verses of "Amazing Grace." As she sang, her father's voice sounded out in her ears. Once they had finished, everyone again took their seats.

The very first line of the sermon began with the question, "Has your life turned out the way that you expected?" A lump began to settle in Stella Mae's throat as her hand slowly moved to her stomach. She felt like his eyes were directly locked with hers. He continued talking about how he thought he would spend his life working at the sawmill like his father did before him. He then went on to talk about how his son, Isaac, passed away at a young age due to illness. "I was crushed," he reminisced, "My son was the light of my life. I fell into a deep depression. I began drinking to try and numb the pain, but nothing could make it go away. Some days, my darling Beth couldn't get me out of bed. Then one day I went to his grave, and I saw this woman kneeling beside his tombstone. I had never seen this woman before in my life. Why was some stranger at my son's grave? *My* son! I ran over to her and demanded to know why she was there. This small, older woman looked up at me with tear-filled eyes as she clutched a small Bible in her hands. She told me that she too had lost her son last year. He drowned playing in the river with his older brothers. She told me she knew the heartbreak that I was feeling."

He had to stop for a moment. Everyone could see he was trying his best to hold back the tears. He managed to gain his composure and continue. "She told me she knew what it felt like to feel like a piece of you was missing. Like you couldn't go on living each day because part of the very thing that made you breathe was gone. Then, slowly, she placed that Bible in my hands. I wasn't a very religious man at the time. I had never really read the Bible, and I didn't attend church. But she looked up at me with those eyes, and she told me that God too knew what it was like to lose a son. After that, I went home that night and read that Bible. I went to church that next Sunday and the next Sunday and the Sunday after that. Finally, God touched something deep inside my heart, and that was when I realized how mad I had been at God. I went up to the altar, and I begged his forgiveness and asked him to save this old boy's soul. Little did I know that just a couple of months after that, God would call me to become a pastor.

Life is never going to turn out the way that we plan it. We are going to have trials to go through and stumbling blocks to overcome. We are going to get mad, have fear, and wonder what in the world we are going to do. It's what we do with that anger and fear and sadness that will lead us to where God wants us to be."

Stella Mae began shifting in her seat as she listened intently to each word from the pastor's mouth. A flutter began to take over in her stomach, a flutter much different from a baby kick. She sat up straight and continued to listen.

The pastor picked up his Bible and began to read scripture. "Proverbs 19:21 says 'There are many devices in a man's heart; nevertheless, the counsel of the Lord, that shall stand.' We don't always know what plan God has for our lives or where we are going to end up. We have to have faith that God is going to bring us to His planned end. When we go against what God has planned for our lives, that is when God is silent. As He says in Psalm 46:10 'Be still and know that I am God: I will be exalted among the heathen, I will be exalted in the earth.' When we are quiet and take time to pray and read our Bible and truly trust and seek God's Will, that is when we hear Him. I had to stop crying out and being angry with God about taking my son and listen to where He was calling me. I never would have guessed that He would lead me to be standing here, in front of all of you, today."

The pastor continued as Stella Mae hung on every word. "I am nothing special. Just because I am standing up here today doesn't mean that God loves me any more than He loves you. I am proof, however, that God can save sinners. I was an angry, alcoholic who would curse and rage and had no desire to learn the things of God. But, He showed me His love for me." Stella Mae's palms began to sweat as her heart rate increased. "And, He can do the same for you. It doesn't matter who you are or what you've done in your life. God loves you. He is going to use you. You are worthy. All you need to do is accept Him and be still. He is calling you."

He asked everyone to rise as he gave the invitation. The melody of the piano felt as if each key were hitting Stella Mae's heart. As she stood there, nails digging into the pew in front of her, her legs trembled. Several people went forward and fell to their knees as they prayed at the altar. With every note of the hymn, Stella Mae's pulse quickened. After several stanzas of contemplation, Stella Mae slowly slid out of the pew and down the center aisle. She was only a few pews back, but the walk seemed like miles. She slowly lowered herself to her knees, a feat to do when she was six months pregnant and had severely swollen ankles. She folded her trembling hands as she bowed her head. Her body began convulsing as she broke down in silent tears.

"Dear God," she began silently, "Forgive me for not praying like I should or going to church like my daddy taught me. I know You are going to use me, Lord. I don't know what you are going to do with a pregnant, uneducated teenager, but I trust You, Lord. Help me to be silent, so I may hear you. Help me to be still so you can take me in your hands and lead me to where You want me. I surrender, God. I surrender all. In Jesus name, I pray. Amen." She remained with her head bowed for a while longer as she silently kept praying and sobbing. Suddenly, an arm draped across her shoulder, and a soft, familiar hand took hers. She slowly turned her head and looked into Mrs. Mayhew's eyes. She slowly pulled her to her side and kissed the side of her head before helping her to her feet. She helped her make her way back to the pew, her hand never leaving Stella Mae's. As they stood there a few heartbeats more, she gave her hand a gentle squeeze as she whispered how she was proud of Stella Mae.

For the first time in a long time, Stella Mae was reminded of two things that day. She smiled and placed her other hand gently and lovingly on her stomach as a calm washed over her. She was reminded of the healing power of a Father and Mother's love.

CHAPTER THIRTEEN

With only three weeks until she was to give birth, Stella Mae found herself constantly exhausted. Her ankles were so swollen she could barely walk. She was having difficulty sleeping at night due to not being able to heave herself from one side to the other. She spent most days in bed reading her Bible and praying that God gives her a safe delivery and a healthy baby. Mrs. Mayhew had her clients meet her at home so she could stay close in the event Stella Mae had the baby.

Every night Stella Mae clutched the picture of her and her father tightly to her chest as she tried to fall asleep. She wanted to raise her baby the way her father had raised her before he died. She wanted to make sure that her baby loved and knew God. She had been practicing singing hymns as she rubbed her belly and prayed out loud for her child. She was going to be the mother that she had always wanted.

One night she woke up in a cold sweat. She began searching frantically for her father's picture. She couldn't find it anywhere. Somehow, she managed to heave herself up and stripped the covers off of the bed. She began screaming and crying, alerting Mrs. Mayhew who came running into the room to see what all of the commotion was about. "I lost him," she cried, "I lost my dad. I have to..." and about that time her stomach began to severely cramp and she felt a warm wet sensation.

"Stella Mae," Mrs. Mayhew shouted excitedly, "your water broke." As Stella Mae's contractions grew closer and closer, Mrs. Mayhew realized that they would have no time to make it to the hospital. This baby was coming whether Stella Mae was ready or not. She quickly tossed all the sheets from the bed and instructed Stella Mae to lay down. Stella Mae reluctantly laid down as she kept screaming in agony. She kept screaming how she needed to find the picture. She had to have it. "There is no time for that now, sweetie. Ready or not, this baby is coming," Mrs. Mayhew hurriedly spoke. Mrs. Mayhew's mother had been a midwife and, thankfully at this moment, her mother had taken her with her to several deliveries. She was worried that she wouldn't remember what to do, but Stella Mae was likely minutes away from being a mother. She busied herself with grabbing towels and warm water. She dipped a rag in cool water and placed it on Stella Mae's sweaty forehead as she told her to breathe. Thankfully, Mrs. Mayhew's mother was a nurse, and she had watched her help deliver countless babies.

Finally, it came time for her to push. "I can't do it. I can't do it," Stella Mae cried and wailed. Mrs. Mayhew took her hand and gave it a reassuring squeeze as she told her that she could. Only a few pushes and she would be holding her precious baby in her arms. Stella Mae closed her eyes and tried her best to picture her father and the grandfather he would have been. She remembered how loving and gentle he was and how he always made her feel safe. She held onto that image of him in her mind as she began to push. She grabbed handfuls of the sheet underneath her as she gripped onto them for dear life. Her hair was a mess from all the sweat, and she had been screaming so loudly her throat started to become hoarse.

After an hour of labor, she had a beautiful baby boy she held tightly to her chest. Her tears of pain had quickly turned to tears of pure love and joy. She took her hand and softly stroked his soft, brown hair as she looked into his innocent crystal blue eyes. Her heart had never felt so full. "I promise," she whispered sweetly in his tiny ear, "to always love and protect you, Nathaniel Jacob Clark." She tenderly kissed his forehead as she closed her eyes, soaking at this moment and longing to freeze time.

"Look what I found," Mrs. Mayhew chirped as she was cleaning up the towels out of the floor. She gently put something in Stella Mae's hand, and she instantly began crying once more.

She looked at the picture of her father, hidden under the bed the entire time, and tearfully whispered as she pulled her son and the photograph close to her chest, "he was here the whole time."

Stella Mae was a wonderful, natural mother. Mrs. Mayhew was worried whether or not Stella Mae would be able to handle things on her own, but she was pleasantly surprised. Stella Mae bathed Nathaniel, nursed him, changed his diapers, sang him to sleep, and would rock him while she read to him from her father's Bible. Mrs. Mayhew couldn't believe how grown up this young woman truly was and what a spirit for God she began developing.

In order to make money to provide for her son, Stella Mae began helping Mrs. Mayhew with her sewing business. When she wasn't working, she was working on her studies and reading any book she could get her hands on so she could obtain her GED. Her passion for learning grew and grew with each flip of the page. She also volunteered down at the church twice a week, helping to feed those who couldn't afford to care for themselves. She loved volunteering and took to it like a natural. When the patrons walked in, their faces immediately lit up upon seeing Stella Mae. They loved her positive attitude and loved it even more when she brought Nathaniel with her to visit. For Stella Mae, life was finally starting to look up, and she felt like she was walking on clouds.

By the time Nathaniel was two, Stella Mae has saved enough money to finally get a place for them to live on their own. She was so excited, yet hated to leave Mrs.

Mayhew, who quickly became a mother figure to her. She loved it when Katherine and her husband would bring their children to visit. She finally felt like a part of a real family. She often wondered what her siblings were doing, more specifically, she worried if they were okay. She wondered if her mother was well, but since Katherine and her family moved away, she may never know.

On the night of Stella Mae's nineteenth birthday, Mrs. Mayhew had cooked a huge dinner to send her off. She fixed chicken, potatoes, green beans, carrots, and rhubarb pie for dessert. They laughed and talked and cried as they recalled their journey together over the three years. Mrs. Mayhew was happy for Stella Mae, but in a way, it was like another one of her daughters was leaving home. She tried her best to smile and be happy on the outside, but on the inside, she was crushed.

Nathaniel was sleeping due to a fever of 102. Stella Mae had been up and down with him the whole night before, and she knew that he needed his rest. After finishing her pie and coffee, she went in to check on him and see if his fever ever broke. As Mrs. Mayhew was clearing the table, she heard Stella Mae let out a panicked squeal. She ran to her room to see her trying to do chest compressions and then took him and cradled him into her arms. Thankfully Dr. Morris lived only two houses down from Mrs. Mayhew's place. Stella Mae nearly knocked Mrs. Mayhew over as she ran out of the house with him tight to her chest as she was screaming and crying. "He's not breathing," she wailed as she threw open the door, "my baby's not breathing."

Mrs. Mayhew sunk down on the couch, stunned and in disbelief. Still clutching the dish towel in her hand, she gripped it with all of her might and bowed her head. "Dear God, please don't let anything happen to that precious little boy. Help Doctor Morris save him. You are the Mighty Physician, Lord. Please, Father, I am begging you.

Put your healing hands on that little boy and his mama.
They need you now, Lord. Now more than ever."

CHAPTER FOURTEEN

Doctor Morris was roused out of bed in the middle of the night by the loudest banging and screaming he had ever heard. *Pretty sure people in Antarctica could have heard the commotion outside my door*, he thought to himself as he grabbed his robe and slippers. He barely had a chance to turn the knob before Stella Mae came bursting through the door in complete and utter distress. "He's not breathing, she kept screaming, "Please, Doctor Morris, you have to help my baby. Do something."

Doctor Morris grabbed him from her arms and carefully laid him on the couch as he began CPR. It took him several minutes, but he was finally able to regain a pulse. He began working quickly to assess what was wrong with Nathaniel. Stella Mae was a sobbing mess, pacing back and forth as she chewed on the skin around her fingernails. "His pulse is very weak," he softly spoke," and I am still worried about his fever being so high that he could stop breathing again. I want to get him to the hospital. All of my tools are there. You can ride in the backseat and hold him until we get there." He walked over and dipped a rag in cool water before handing it to Stella Mae. "Keep this pressed against his forehead."

Stella Mae did exactly as she was told. She tried her best to take deep breaths and calm down, but her child was practically dying in her arms. She wanted so badly for him to open his eyes so she knew that he would be okay. To her avail, they remained closed. Not even the slightest flutter. She wasted no time in throwing open the door as soon as they pulled into a spot outside of the hospital. Doctor Morris was quickly behind her opening the door and grabbing him from her arms as he laid him in one of the hospital beds. He immediately began covering his body in cold compresses to bring his fever down and covered his face with an oxygen mask.

Doctor Morris listened intently to Nathaniel's breathing, and a look of panic flashed across his face. As he removed his stethoscope, he released a deep sigh. "Stella Mae, why don't we go over here and have a seat while we let Nathaniel rest," he whispered as he motioned for her to sit in the chairs outside his room. Stella Mae reluctantly took a seat, but she couldn't take her eyes off of her poor baby boy. That bed made him look so small. His face looked like porcelain, and he was lying so still it was as if he were a doll, like the ones she used to tuck into her bed as a child. Doctor Morris rubbed the back of his neck and let out a deep sigh before turning to face Stella Mae. "Stella Mae, look, I, I don't really know how to tell you this. Based on what I've seen, I'm afraid Nathaniel has developed tuberculosis." His words hung heavy in the air and echoed in Stella Mae's ears.

"You, you can save him, right," she managed to squeak out in between the tears. Her entire body was trembling, and her hands were slick with sweat.

The saddened look in Doctor Morris's eyes spoke volumes. He tried to seem optimistic, but he couldn't hide the uncertainty in his voice. "Stella Mae, I'm not going to lie to you. In the last six months, I've seen eight cases of tuberculosis. They all had the same symptoms as Nathaniel…" his voice trailed off as he glanced over at the tiny, innocent boy fighting for his life in that big hospital bed.

"You were able to help them though, weren't you," she asked with hope in her voice. She needed hope. She desperately needed something to hold onto. Something to keep her going because all she wanted to do right now was give her life for her son. That hope quickly faded as she saw the tears standing behind Doctor Morris's eyes.

She buried her face in her hands as her body heaved from the sobs as Doctor Morris responded, "No, I'm sorry. I couldn't save them."

Stella Mae spent every minute she could at the hospital as she held Nathaniel's hand. Her mask she was forced to wear in order to be around him had practically become a part of her. She was starting to look like a bag of bones since she had lost at least ten pounds. She refused to eat, to sleep, to do anything besides stay by her son's side. For a week, she watched as the tiniest little puffs of breath escaped from her son's lungs. The medicine wasn't helping, and Nathaniel was growing weaker by the day.

On one Sunday afternoon after church, Mrs. Mayhew stopped by to bring Stella Mae some lunch and to check on how Nathaniel was doing. As she sat the basket down and put on her mask, Stella Mae informed her she wasn't hungry. Mrs. Mayhew sat down in a chair on the other side of the bed. She caressed Nathaniel's check and told Stella Mae not to stress and worry. "God will protect him, Stella Mae," she replied, "He will heal him. You just need to be pa..."

She was cut off by Stella Mae flying into a rage. "He will heal him? He will protect him? If He was going to protect him, He wouldn't have allowed him to get sick in the first place. You've always told me God provides for us. How is it providing to first take my father from me and to bring that awful man into our lives? Then on top of that, he is now taking my son, the only thing good in my life," her body was shaking in anger. "How is that providing? You've lied to me. This whole time. You have done nothing but lie to me. So, please, just do me a favor and leave my son and me alone." With that, she turned and bolted out the door, slamming it so hard behind her; it caused Mrs. Mayhew to jump. She sat there a few moments more in a state of disbelief. Silent tears escaped her eyes as she looked at Nathaniel, still sleeping and not moving the slightest muscle at his mother's outburst.

She took his tiny hand in hers and put it to her lips, hidden behind the mask. She closed her eyes and allowed more tears to slip. Then, she began to pray, "Father, I know she didn't mean those things. She is angry right now, and I know that. Help her, Father. She needs you. This precious boy needs you. You can heal them, Lord. You can heal them both. They desperately need you, Lord. If what she needs right now is for me to stay away, I will. But, God, what she really needs right now is You. She needs you now more than ever. Lead her back to You. Be with them, God. In the precious name of Jesus, I pray. Amen."

As she opened her eyes, a ray of sunlight fell on Nathaniel's body. She broke down into tears as she held his hand to her chest, for she knew in her heart of hearts that warmth and Light was not the sun, but the Son.

CHAPTER FIFTEEN

Stella Mae wandered around town for several hours trying to calm herself down. Who was Mrs. Mayhew to be talking about how great her God is when her son was dying? For all she knew, he was probably already gone. He was barely breathing when she left, she just knew that he had been taken from her. She had wanted so badly believe what she had been hearing in church and she knew her father would want her to have faith that God would bring her through this, but how could she have faith when He had taken her father from her and left her with her mother? Left her with the responsibility of having to take care of her brothers and sisters or they would never have been taken care of? Left her with the responsibility of raising herself because her mother couldn't leave the side of her alcoholic and abusive husband? And now, He was about to take the life of her beautiful, innocent baby boy. She just couldn't take it anymore. She couldn't go back there to see her son's lifeless body. Her only option was to leave and never look back.

She finally came to an alley where she saw two young women, both tall, skinny blondes dressed in short, racy dresses with high heels passing a brown paper bag to one another. Stella Mae tried to hide in the shadows but was unsuccessful.

"Take a picture, it'll last longer," the first tall, skinny blonde girl rasped. Her voice sounded like she ate a bowl of nails and tacks for breakfast. She placed her hand on her bony hip and looked Stella Mae up and down. "Get a load of this one, Raz. Looks like she just walked out of a department store ad," she snorted. The other blonde, Raz, smiled a nervous, forced smile. She wasn't as bone-thin as the other one, and to be honest, she looked as much out of place as Stella Mae did. "You just gonna stand there kid or are ya gonna do somethin'," the raspy blonde barked.

Stella Mae slowly walked toward the two women, her legs shaking like a plate full of Jello. She nervously replied, " I, I'm sorry. I've just been walking around town, and then I saw you two down the alley and I jus…"

"Gotta name, kid," the tall one demanded.

"Ste…Stella Mae," she managed with her voice trembling as much as her knees.

The tall blonde let out a snort. "Name's Evie, and this is Raz. What's a goody two shoes like you doing walking around this late at night?"

Stella Mae swallowed deeply; her heart was seconds from beating out of her chest. "I just, I just needed to get away from someone. She was suffocating me, and I just couldn't take it anymore." Not meaning to, Stella Mae started to cry. Raz quickly rushed to her side, pulling her into her shoulder and shushing her.

"It's okay," Raz warmly spoke. Her voice was soft and comforting, the way someone would talk back home. She stroked the back of Stella Mae's head as she tried to assure her that everything was going to be okay and to get her to calm down.

Evie rolled her eyes and pulled out a cigarette. "You can tell us anything," she gave a coy smile as she let out a breath of smoke and tossed her lighter back in her cheetah-print purse, "We're pretty good at keeping secrets."

Stella Mae tried to gain control of herself. She used the sleeve of her sweater to wipe her eyes and took several deep breaths as she choked on Evie's smoke. Once she was able to speak, she quietly explained, "Someone, someone I care deeply about is dying. Then this, this woman who thinks that she knows me, and my life is trying to tell me to have faith and to have hope. How am I supposed to do that when people that I love just keep dying?" Her quiet tears quickly turned to loud, angry sobs that echoed throughout the whole alley.

Raz pulled her closer to her and wrapped her arms around her as tightly as she could. Stella Mae knew this woman was a stranger, but she felt comfort in her arms. Evie stood with a heel against the wall as she took the last drag of her cigarette and a long drink from the paper bag as she tossed the butt into a nearby puddle. She stumbled over to Stella Mae and thrust the bottle in her face. "Here kid, this'll make you feel better," she growled.

Stella Mae held the bottle with uncertainty in her hands. She saw a flicker of worry in Raz's eyes. Thoughts of her father, his casket and the echoes of the shotguns that still bring fear into her chest, the cries of her siblings, the deathlike look of her son in that hospital bed and that feeling of helplessness knowing that there was nothing to do. She remembered what had happened the last time she was in a situation like this and how she should have said no, but she also wanted her mind to be as numb as her heartfelt. She took a long drink from the bag and coughed as the liquid burned her throat. Once she caught her breath, she took another long drink. Her head started to spin, but she allowed herself to give in as she continued chugging. Evie gave her a slap on the back as she laughed, "Hey, this kid might not be so bad after all. Stick with us, kiddo. We'll help make all that pain go away."

Stella Mae noticed a slight wince from Raz, and worry settled into her face. A little voice told her to stop, but she couldn't stop the reel playing in her mind. She saw Nathaniel's ghostly pale face flash into her mind, and she closed her eyes for a brief second. She took another long drink and then used her sleeve to wipe her mouth, the corners of which had turned into a nervous smile. She longed to feel numb, but little did she know that her decision that day would cause her to feel anything but numb.

Stella Mae forced herself to push Nathaniel from her mind. She just knew that by now Mrs. Mayhew had planned a little ceremony and her son was gone. She couldn't allow herself to go through another funeral of someone that she loved. She loved her son, but her heart was devoid of faith and hope. She had been with Evie and Raz for two months now. They were staying in a little rundown house on the outskirts of town. Stella Mae found a job working in a diner during the day while Evie and Raz stayed out all night. Most nights by the time that they came home Stella Mae would be passed out in her bed still clutching a bottle of whatever Raz and Evie had in the house. Her sober days were few and far between.

She was a completely different person since she started hanging around her new friends. She spent most of her days in a drunken stupor and, after finding Evie's stash of pills, lost about twenty pounds and was now even bonier than Evie. She cut off her long, blonde waves and her once beautiful hair now barely touched her bony shoulders. Her cheeks were sunken in, and all evidence of happiness had vanished from her life. She woke up in the middle of the night every night screaming as she dreamed of her father and her son. Her body would be covered in sweat and her heart racing. She would grab the nearest bottle and chug until she couldn't breathe. She shared a room with Raz, and she would always rush over to her bed and pull her into her arms until she calmed down. She would sit beside her on the bed until she would fall back to sleep. Raz had become the older sister that she never had and never knew she needed.

One night, in particular, Stella Mae had gone on a serious bender. She probably had enough drugs in her system to kill a circus elephant. She was sick for hours on end. Raz held her hair back and would put a cool rag on her forehead as they both laid on the cool tile floor. Raz was four years older than Stella Mae, and she felt the need to protect her. She wished Stella Mae had just kept walking that night and that she never would have ended up with this life. She reminded her so much of her own little sister, AnnaLee, who died when she was twelve years old. After that, Raz ran away from home and fell in with Evie after living on the streets for six months. She didn't want to follow after Evie, with the drinking and the strange men, but she felt like she owed the person who had saved her from dying in an alley.

Sometime during the night, Raz had fallen asleep. She stirred slightly and carefully as to not wake Stella Mae who was asleep on her lap. Raz decided to try and wake her to give her some water to hydrate. She softly stroked her hair and whispered her name, but no response. She gave her shoulder a gentle nudge, but there was no movement. Stricken with fear, she began crying and screaming her name as she shook her, still getting no response. She checked her pulse and found not even the slightest beat.

Immediately, she began CPR, trying desperately to keep track of the compressions as she sobbed with each chest thrust. She still couldn't regain a pulse. She filled up a cup and splashed the water in her face, but still nothing. She rested on her knees and pushed her hair back with her hands. Then, she took her fists and hit them as hard as she could on Stella Mae's chest as she let out an exhausted scream. As she laid her head on Stella Mae's chest in defeat, she began to hear a faint heartbeat. She immediately checked her pulse and pulled her into her chest as she sobbed so hard, she could barely breathe. It took all the strength that she had to drag her from the bathroom to the couch.

She ran outside and started pounding on the door of her neighbor, Mr. Reynolds. She pounded so hard she thought she was going to put her fist through the door. A sleepy-eyed and confused Mr. Reynolds opened the door. He was an elderly man who lost his wife several years ago. Raz would go every so often and help him out around the house and sometimes cook him meals. "Mr. Reynolds, please. It's an emergency. I need to borrow your car," she blurted out in a panic, "my friend is dying. I have to get her to the hospital."

Mr. Reynolds hobbled over to the table to retrieve his keys. "I hope your friend will be okay," he sweetly managed to croak.

She thanked him and rushed back over to her house. Between the fear and the worry, her adrenaline was going a mile a minute and she managed to find the strength to carry Stella Mae out to the car and lay her gently in the backseat. She then ran around to the driver's seat and threw the car in drive. The tires let out the loudest shriek she had ever heard, and she was sure that she woke the entire neighborhood. Her foot pressed the gas pedal all the way down to the floor as she flew down the road to the hospital. It was only a seven-minute drive, although she made it in four, but it felt like endless hours had passed.

She finally slammed the car into park outside the hospital and hurried to pull Stella Mae from the backseat. She cradled her in her arms as she carried her through the hospital doors. "Help, please! Someone help her," she screamed and cried as she frantically tried to find someone. A man came rushing to her side and grabbed Stella Mae from her arms. He hurried her over to a hospital bed and began working on her. "She has no pulse. Starting CPR," the doctor informed his nurse. After delivering chest compressions for several minutes, the doctor shouted that she still had no pulse and to grab the paddles. "Clear," his deep voice boomed as he delivered the shock. Raz became nearly inconsolable as she watched Stella Mae's body shoot into the air and back down onto the table. Her screams of fear echoed throughout the emergency room. A nurse came over and gently put her arms on her shoulders and led her away from Stella Mae's bed, where she was still receiving electric shocks. The loud alarm of the monitors rang continuously in her ears.

The nurse led her to the waiting room and tried her best to calm her down. She got her a cup of water, and she was eventually able to take a couple of sips. She paced back and forth for hours waiting to hear something from the doctor. What could be taking them so long? She needed answers. Finally, the doctor came out rubbing his face with his hands. He looked exhausted, completely drained. He motioned for her to sit down in a chair in the waiting room. Her hands began to tremble as she folded them on her lap. "She's stable, for now," the doctor informed her. She let out a sigh of relief as the need to cry began to come over her again.

"Ca- can I see her," she choked.

The doctor gave her a reassuring smile and told her to follow him. Stella Mae looked so young lying in that hospital bed. She had an oxygen mask helping her to breathe and several IVs in her arm. Raz made her way over to the chair beside her and sat down as she took her hand in hers, holding it just under her chin. Stella Mae was still unconscious. "We expect her to make a full recovery," the doctor offered warmly, "she's lucky she has a friend like you. If you had been any later, she wouldn't have made it. You saved her life."

"No," Raz smiled as she sucked back the tears and kissed Stella Mae's hand, "she saved mine."

CHAPTER SIXTEEN

Stella Mae remained in the hospital for three days, with Raz never leaving her side. Evie stopped by for a few minutes on the second day long enough to pick up the rent money from Raz. Her eyes were glazed over, and her hair looked like she hadn't washed it in weeks. She snatched the money from her hands, turned on her faded heels, and half stumbled out of the hospital room.

Stella Mae and Raz sat there eating bags of vending machine chips and laughing with one another. It sounded more like a slumber party than a hospital visitation. "Thanks for staying with me, Raz," Stella Mae gently and genuinely spoke, "I would be dead right now if it weren't for you."

"Bella," she replied as she dusted the chips from her fingers, "it's Bella. Bella Savannah Wilkes. Raz is my work name. I didn't feel comfortable with all those strange guys knowing my real name. So, I decided to change it."

"How did you even get into that business," Stella Mae asked inquisitively. "I mean you don't really seem like the kind of person who could be a..."

"You mean a harlot? A jezebel? A lady of the night? Trust me, I've heard them all before." Raz got up from her chair and started pacing the length of the room. Stella Mae pulled herself up, so she was sitting up straight in bed. "After my little sister, AnnaLee, died, I was a mess. My parents were a mess. They shut down completely. I became invisible to them. They didn't even notice that I had left. For a while, I was living on the streets, digging through trash to find food or going weeks at a time with nothing to eat." She pulled her hair back from her face for a moment as she held it behind her head and took several deep breaths.

68

She dropped her hair and continued, "Then, Evie came along and found me. She said that she could give me a warm place to stay, food to eat, and a way to make money. I didn't know exactly what she meant, but it was either accept her offer or face impending death. I was facing another winter on the streets. I felt like I owed her, you know. I mean, I'm still alive today because of her. Do I like what I do? Not at all. But I can't leave Evie. Not after what she's done for me. So, I just close my eyes and make myself go numb."

Stella Mae felt tears behind her eyes. "But you don't have to. You can get out of there. Find a different job. Come work with me at the diner. You don't have to live this kind of life. You don't owe Evie anything. She treats you like trash. You don't deserve to be treated like that. You deserve better. I mean the way you've treated me. This isn't you."

"I know," Raz squeaked as she began to cry. "I just, I can't leave her. Not after all she's done for me." She then began to breakdown into tears.

About the time that Stella Mae was getting up to go over to her, a tiny voice rang out in her room. Stella Mae's heart stopped at the familiar sound, and she broke out in uncontrollable tears.

"Mommy!"

She couldn't believe her eyes. Had she just been in a coma and dreaming this whole time? Was she still in a drunken and drug-induced stupor? "Mommy," the precious voice rang out again. She wrapped her arms as tightly as she could around her son. Her *son*! The son that she thought she had lost. The son that she realized now that had abandoned. The son who was alive and well and, in her arms, making all the broken pieces whole again.

69

Mrs. Mayhew was beside her bed with a look that was a heartbreaking mixture of happiness, relief, and worry. "Mrs. Mayhew," Stella Mae choked, "wh...wha...how"?

"It took a couple of days, but the medicine finally started to work. It took him about three weeks to build his strength back up. He asked for you every day. You were his first word as he woke up," Mrs. Mayhew replied through tears. Stella Mae held her son tightly to her chest too afraid to let go. If this was a dream, she never wanted to wake up. "Come home, Stella Mae," Mrs. Mayhew whispered, "come home."

"I don't deserve to come back after the way I treated you. I'm so sorry. I was so terrible to you, and you were just trying to help me and encourage me. I'm so sorry." Mrs. Mayhew only hushed her and told her all was forgiven and that she understood. She reminded her that all she wanted was for Stella Mae to come home. To be with her son. To be safe and to know that she was loved.

Stella Mae looked over to Bella, who was standing sheepishly in the corner of the room trying to dry her own eyes. "Mrs. Mayhew, this is Bella," she smiled through her tears as she gestured over in her direction. Bella smiled warmly as she wiped a tear from her cheek. "Bella, this is Mrs. Mayhew and this," she tickled her son's belly as he let out a heartwarming giggle, "is my son, Nathaniel."

Bella made her way over beside Stella Mae. "Hi, Nathaniel," she warmly greeted him and received a warm smile in return. Sadness quickly overtook her face as she realized Stella Mae would likely be leaving to go home.

Stella Mae took Bella's hand and gave it a gentle squeeze. "Come with us," she whispered pleadingly, "Please. You can have a better life. You deserve a better life. Just come with us. You owe Evie nothing. You're the one who does all the cooking and the cleaning, and you

70

don't receive even so much as a thank you. She may have saved you from living on the streets, but it's up to you to save you from yourself." Bella looked over to Mrs. Mayhew whose face was full of warmth and assurance. She gave her a welcoming smile and nodded her head as she told her she would love for her to join them. Suddenly, a tiny hand reached for her free hand, and she looked down into the face of a precious little boy whose innocent eyes beamed at her. She looked into Stella Mae's pleading eyes as Stella Mae again whispered, "Do it for your sister."

Bella closed her eyes and allowed the tears to squeeze through. She saw her sister's face. Her big doe eyes that glowed like emeralds dancing on a cloud and her soft honey hair that she always had hanging down in her eyes until Bella would braid it back in ribbons. She thought of the innocence her sister held and how much her death had destroyed her. Her little sister had looked up to her, practically idolized her. What would her sister think of what she was doing if she could see her now? As she opened her eyes, she saw the pleading on the three faces in front of her, and before she knew she was thinking it, her mouth spoke her heart.

"Yes, I'll go with you."

CHAPTER SEVENTEEN

Stella Mae sat in the passenger seat and watched as they drove back into town. Her face lit up as she passed all of her favorite buildings. The old bookstore on the corner where she would spend her Saturday afternoons. The bakery where she would go get cranberry muffins after church on Sundays. The cobblestone church where she had accepted Christ as her Savior. And the hospital where she had railed against Him. As they passed by, her heart sank and began to race within her chest.

She became confused as they drove past their old house. "Wait, you passed the house," she blurted.

"That's not where we live anymore," Mrs. Mayhew replied with a smile. They drove another minute down the road, and the car came to a stop. "This," she smiled, "is your new home."

Stella Mae opened the car door and stepped out into the warmth of the sun. She stood in awe of the beautiful house. Before her stood a beautiful farmhouse with gorgeous chestnut wood and a cobblestone path leading to the beautifully decorated front door. The front of the house was lined with an explosion of beautiful and radiant colorful flowers. As she stood and took everything in, her precious little boy ran over and grabbed her hand. She picked him up and gave him a kiss on the cheek before he laid his head on her shoulder.

"Do you like it," Mrs. Mayhew giggled at the mesmerized look on Stella Mae's face.

Stella Mae let out a warm giggle and turned to face Mrs. Mayhew. "Are you kidding me, it's incredible," she blurted.

"It was my father's. Once my husband passed away, and Katherine moved out, living in this big house was just too much. I had been renting it out for a couple of years, but the family that was staying there moved away. I figured with Nathaniel getting older, it would be nice to have some more space for him to explore. Plus, I hadn't given up hope of finding you. Now, I have this beautiful family to once again fill this house with love and laughter," she smiled. She tried to hide the fact that she was on the verge of tears, but that became impossible as Stella Mae threw her arms around her and wrapped her in the biggest embrace she could handle. Nathaniel wrapped his tiny arms around her neck as the three stood there embracing.

Stella Mae opened her eyes and saw Bella at the back of the car unloading bags. She called her over and pulled her into the pile. "This," she managed as she sucked in her tears, "is the greatest family anyone could ever ask for." She never wanted to let go. For the first time in a long time, all of the broken pieces felt like they were finally coming together, yet, she felt something was missing.

She walked down the cobblestone pathway and opened the door. Amazement abounded in her as she took in the farmhouse beauty before her. It was the kind of home she only thought she could ever dream of. Bella stood beside her taking in the sheer beauty of this wonderful home she was would be living in. It sure beat living in a rundown two bedroom house with an alcoholic and drug addict, whether she did rescue her or not. "You have a beautiful home," Bella uttered in amazement.

Mrs. Mayhew appeared behind her and lovingly placed a hand on her shoulder. "This is your home too, dear," Mrs. Mayhew smiled as Stella Mae smiled in return before reaching out to give Bella's hand a loving and reassuring squeeze. She hadn't had a "home" since she left her parents after her sister died. For the first time, she finally felt like someone truly cared for her. She finally felt like part of a family.

They all went off exploring the house, which was beautifully decorated and so much more than any of them could have ever imagined. Stella Mae came to Nathaniel's room, decorated in a western theme, and stood in amazement. Nathaniel ran in the room and started playing with his toys and calling for Stella Mae to come to play with him. She got down on the floor and helped him build with his blocks, and Bella came and joined them. Every time they would build the tower up so high that it would crash, Nathaniel would let out this belly laugh that reminded Stella Mae so much of her father that it gave her chills.

After a while, Stella Mae told Bella to keep an eye on Nathaniel so she could run to the restroom. Bella was more than happy to stay and play with that bright, beautiful little boy. Stella Mae went down the hallway and saw the bathroom was right at the end of the hall. As she made her way down the wooden hall, she stopped and noticed the bedroom beside Nathaniel's. She felt drawn into the room by this feeling in her chest she could never quite describe. The bed was covered in a beautiful lacy cover, and a chair sat at the foot of the bed beside a bookcase full of her favorite books. Pictures were hung on the wall of her and Nathaniel when he was a baby, some while she was away, and pictures of her with the Mayhew family. The picture that made her heart stop was the one in a beautiful frame on the nightstand. One that had protected her through giving birth, one that had kept memories alive, one that she had left behind when she ran away from her son. She picked the picture up as she sat on the bed and the tears began to ceaselessly flow down her cheeks. Her father holding her up in the air was beautifully encased in that frame, along with his memory that was encased in her heart.

She closed her eyes together as she tried to make the tears stop. Suddenly, familiar arms were wrapping her in an embrace. "I know how much that picture means to you," Mrs. Mayhew gently offered, "I wanted to make sure that it was kept someplace safe." She held Stella Mae's head to her shoulder as she gently stroked her hair and softly hushed. "I have something else I believe belongs to you," she smiled as she reached into the nightstand and pulled out her father's Bible. Stella Mae took it in her hands and caressed the worn edges. She pulled it tight to her chest with the picture frame and closed her eyes as she took a deep breath.

As she opened her eyes, she turned to face a smiling Mrs. Mayhew. "I, I don't think I can go back," Stella Mae's voice shook, "I can't go back into that church. What will people think of me? They'll never forgive me for abandoning my son? How could God ever even forgive me when I turned my back on Him?"

Mrs. Mayhew's smile faded as a look of sadness came over her face. "Stella Mae," she began sweetly, "you do know why Christ died on the cross, don't you? To forgive us of all of our sins. There is nothing that you can ever do that Christ will not forgive you for. Those people in that church, do you want to know what their prayer is every service? For you to come home. They just want you safe and happy. They were never angry or disappointed with you. They love you. You are a part of our family. They won't forgive you; they have nothing to forgive you for."

Stella Mae broke down in uncontrollable sobs. Mrs. Mayhew did her very best to console her, but there was no use. "I. Just. Can't. Face. Them," she heaved in between each word.

Mrs. Mayhew pulled her in close to her chest and told her that she understood. "Just promise me that you'll consider coming back when you're ready," she warmly pleaded. Stella Mae nodded her head reluctantly and tried with all her might to stop crying.

Lord, what is it going to take for this little girl to forgive herself and to feel your forgiveness, Mrs. Mayhew prayed silently. Little did she know that within the next few weeks, she would find that answer, whether she wanted to hear it or not.

CHAPTER EIGHTEEN

The newly formed Mayhew household had settled into a routine quite nicely. Bella found a job helping out at the local cafe, and Stella Mae started working at the bookstore. Mrs. Mayhew had begun working fewer and fewer hours since she had come down with a terrible cold that she couldn't seem to shake. Thankfully Mr. Harold, the owner of the bookstore, allowed Stella Mae to bring Nathaniel with her to work. His wife typically came by during the day to help out with the books, and she would watch Nathaniel while Mrs. Mayhew stayed home and rested. She was so thankful to have such a supportive community behind her. She finally gained back the weight that she had lost from all the drugs, and she felt better than she had in months. She celebrated her twentieth birthday a couple weeks ago and managed to finish all the credits she needed to get her GED. Things were finally looking up for Stella Mae and her little family.

Nathaniel's third birthday party was only a few days away. Stella Mae spent all of her time on her break planning the perfect party for her son. The last few weeks had felt like she hadn't missed any time at all with him, yet she was gone for nearly a year. She couldn't shake that guilt or shame from her conscience. She tried her best to make every single tiny moment count to make up for her absence. For Stella Mae, it was imperative that she plan the perfect party for her beautiful son.

On Friday night she stayed up decorating the house for Saturday. She hung streamers, blew up balloons, and put the finishing touches on his cake shaped like a little, brown puppy. She worked for hours and hours to make sure that the cake was absolutely perfect. Saturday morning, she made puppy-shaped chocolate chip pancakes and freshly squeezed orange juice. Nathaniel practically inhaled three pancakes before Stella Mae had to cut him off.

By the time that the afternoon came, and it was time for the party, Nathaniel was bouncing off the walls with excitement. He ran all around the yard with his friends and gorged himself on pizza and chips. He was the happiest little boy in the world, and everyone was all smiles watching how well their children played together. It truly was the most perfect birthday party that any parent could ever ask for. Mrs. Mayhew had spent most of the party in her room still not feeling well but managed the strength to come out of her room to watch Nathaniel blow out the candles on his cake.

Everyone began to sing "Happy birthday" as Stella Mae brought out the cake. The candles on the cake were nothing compared to the light in Nathaniel's eyes, the light of pure happiness. Mrs. Mayhew's heart began to race, and a tightness in her chest caused her to become short of breath. Stella Mae was so focused on Nathaniel's excitement; she hadn't noticed that Mrs. Mayhew's face had gone white as a ghost. Her heart began racing even faster and faster until it stopped. As soon as the last word of "Happy Birthday" was sung, Mrs. Mayhew collapsed to the ground. Stella Mae rushed over to her and tried to wake her up. She was screaming her name as she held her head in her lap and yelling for someone to call an ambulance.

The sound of the sirens still echoed in her ears as the rest of the world fell silent. Her own heart stopped as she watched the paramedics load Mrs. Mayhew into the ambulance. The ambulance pulled off and all Stella Mae could do is drop to her knees and hold her crying son as Bella tried her best to console his crying mother.

Bella tried her hardest to talk Stella Mae into going with her to the hospital, but Stella Mae couldn't bring herself to go. She couldn't look at Mrs. Mayhew looking as helpless as Nathaniel once had, or worse, she couldn't bear to go say goodbye to a lifeless body. That woman had practically saved her life, and now she was on the verge of death, and there was nothing that Stella Mae could do. She felt so small, so helpless. Bella decided that she needed to go see her and make sure everything was okay. With the state Stella Mae was in, she volunteered to take Nathaniel with her, to which Stella Mae had no objections.

Stella Mae paced the living room for 45 minutes, paying no attention to the mess that was left to clean up from the party. She felt like she was suffocating. She needed air. She grabbed her jacket and decided that she needed a walk. She walked around town for about an hour before her feet led her to the doors of the church. That beautiful stone church that now struck fear and shame in the pit of her stomach. She slowly opened the door and made her way inside before setting down in a pew on the back row. She wasn't sure how she ended up here of all places, but something deep inside her told her this was where she needed to be.

She placed her arms on the pew in front of her and buried her face as she sobbed uncontrollably. Suddenly, a soft hand touched her on the back and caused her to jump. She looked up into the eyes of Reverend Bower and felt flushed with shame and embarrassment. Her face turned a thousand shades of red as she tried to avoid making direct eye contact with him. "Stella Mae," his caring voice began, "I'm so happy to see you. Is everything okay?"

Stella Mae could only shake her head. She couldn't find the words to express what she was feeling. To be honest, she wasn't completely sure that she knew exactly what was going on inside of her. Reverend Bower sat down in the pew in front of her and turned around to face her. "I heard about what happened to Mrs. Mayhew. That couldn't have been easy to watch," he spoke with concern.

"It's my fault," Stella Mae sobbed, "it's my fault this happened. Everyone I have ever cared about has either died or came close to dying. I loved my father, and he's gone. I love my Nathaniel, and he nearly died in my arms. I love Mrs. Mayhew and she..." Stella Mae couldn't control the sobbing any longer. In between heaves she blurted, "I left them. I left all of them and now this, this is my punishment. I don't deserve happiness. I left her to take care of Nathaniel all on her own and I..." she trailed off and closed her eyes for several seconds, afraid to look Reverend Bower in the eyes. She finally managed to look him in the eye for a brief second as she shamefully admitted, "I turned my back on God, and this is what I get. I lose the one person who gave up everything for me and who saved me."

Reverend Bower pulled a handkerchief from his pocket and gave it to Stella Mae as he warmly offered, "There is someone else who gave up everything and saved you, Stella Mae. Christ gave His life for you so that you can be saved. He is not punishing you. He doesn't hate you, and He is not angry with you. He wants you to come home. He wants you to know that He forgives you and that He loves you. He wants you to accept Him. The Bible says that God is not willing that any should perish. None of this, your father, Nathaniel's sickness, what happened to Mrs. Mayhew, none of it is your fault. Sometimes, we wander, and we stray from God. But, Stella Mae, He will welcome you back home. Matthew 11:28 says, 'Come unto me, all ye that labour and are heavy laden, and I will give you rest.' Let Him give you rest, Stella Mae. Let Him help you carry your burdens."

She knew he was right, but she still couldn't shake the feeling that all of this was somehow her fault. "But," she hung her head as she tried to force the tears to stop, "how do you make it go away? The guilt. The pain. That feeling in the pit of your stomach that the people you care most about in this world are better off without you because all you do is cause them pain and suffering."

Reverend Bower sat silently for a few moments trying to find the words to console her. "Do you remember the sermon I gave your first Sunday here when I talked about my son," he asked her as he stood up to pull his wallet from his pocket. From it, he took out an old, faded picture. "This is my little boy. As you know, I was lost after we lost him. Devastated. I didn't feel like I should live anymore. Why should I live when my innocent son didn't get that chance? Do you know what I learned that day from the woman in the cemetery?"

Stella Mae sheepishly made eye contact with him as she tried to force her eyes open through her tears. "I learned that it wasn't about my pain. It was about my son and what he would have wanted. He would have wanted me to be happy. He would have wanted me to do something to help others. That led me into the ministry and going to church. That first church service I attended nearly broke me. Know what I realized? It wasn't me being punished by God. It was God trying to get my attention. It was God trying to tell me that I needed to change some things in my life and that I was missing something. My wife and I had money, we had a nice house and good jobs. What I didn't have was Christ. When I accepted Him, man, things changed. I was the happiest I had been since my son died. I'll never forget the day that I accepted Christ. We left church that afternoon and drove home. My wife and I were completely silent. The radio was on a Christian station she always loved to listen to. Now, my boy's favorite animal was a Blue Jay. He loved absolutely loved them. His room was covered in them, he read about them all the time, and that was the name of his little league team. In my mind on my drive home, I kept thinking about the commitment I made to God. I turned to my wife and thanked her for everything and for never giving up on me. She told me that our son would pray for me to get saved every night. Not a minute later, a blue jay flies by our window. I smiled thinking of my little boy. But then, as soon as that bird flew by the song 'How Great Our Father's Love For Us' came on the radio, and I lost it. I like to think that was my boy's way of saying that he would see me soon. I know I am going to see my boy some day and I know that I am worth more than what I thought of myself back then. Stella Mae, you are worth more than rubies and diamonds. You are more than your mistakes. You are worthy of being loved, and you are loved. By God, by Nathaniel, by Mrs. Mayhew, and by this whole community. You need to accept the love of Christ. Through His love and his forgiveness, you will love yourself."

Stella Mae trembled in fear and conviction. She felt this deep need inside of her. Something that had long been missing. A void she thought she could fill with drinking and drugs. A void she thought she could fill with her son and being a good mother. A void that no matter what she did, she could not fill. She tried her eyes with her sleeve and looked up to meet his eyes. She drew in a long, deep breath and finally exhaled. "I'm ready," she replied shakily at first, "I'm ready to accept Him as my Lord and Savior." The longer she prayed with Reverend Bower, the more the sadness and fear began to melt away from her. For the first time, she felt like she could breathe. She felt a happiness inside of her that she had never felt before in her life. The tears of heartache and total despair turned to cries of jubilation.

For the first time in her life, Stella Mae finally knew Who had been missing from that void, and that void would never again be felt.

CHAPTER NINETEEN

Stella Mae walked out of the doors of the church and felt the warmth of the sunlight on her face. The smile on her face would not fade. She felt a joy in her that she had only ever dreamed about. As she hailed a cab to take her to the hospital, she thought of Mrs. Mayhew and begged God to let her be alive. To just let her be okay, please, just let her be okay.

The cab pulled up in front of the hospital, and Stella Mae sat there trying to gather her courage. She got out and made her way ever so slowly through the doors and to the nurse's station. They directed her to room 226 and, with her hand on the handle, she froze. She looked through the small window in the door to see Mrs. Mayhew lying in the bed, an oxygen mask on her face and numerous IVs in her arms. Her eyes were closed, and her face looked sunken and pale. She looked over to see Bella in the chair beside the bed. She noticed her and quietly got up and exited the room. Bella embraced her in a terrifying hug. "Where have you been," she demanded with worry, "I was getting worried about you?"

"I'm sorry, I just needed some air," Stella Mae replied with sadness in her voice. They stayed in an embrace for a while as Stella Mae yet again searched for the courage to walk through that door. She finally pulled back and faced Bella. "Where's Nathaniel," she asked as she fought the urge to cry.

"I took him to the nursery. He was ready for a nap, and I didn't want her to be alone or for him to wake her," Bella replied. Stella Mae agreed she made the right call. She looked through the door again and stared for several seconds at the incredible woman in that bed. She felt Bella reach out and give her hand a reassuring squeeze. She smiled and told her that she would give them some time together.

Stella Mae quietly and slowly opened the door and entered the room. What seemed like a thousand years had passed by the time she made it to the chair beside the bed and slowly took a seat. Her trembling hands took Mrs. Mayhew's as she stared at the frail body in that bed. Mrs. Mayhew gave no sign of acknowledgment that Stella Mae was there. "Hey," she softly began, "it's me. Stella Mae." She gave an awkward, nervous laugh. "I'm uh, I'm sorry I'm just now getting here but," she let out a deep sigh, "I was, I was lost. I think I've been lost all my life and I didn't know how to find my way. But, uh, I ran into Reverend Bower. I can't really explain it, but I somehow ended up at the church. Anyway, I got to talking to him, and I realized something. I realized why I felt so lost, why I couldn't find my way." Stella Mae's hands became wet with perspiration, and the trembling of her hands was that of a seismic scale. "I realized that it wasn't my way I should have been looking for, I needed to be looking for God's way."

She tried her best to fight it, but her tears won out. She broke down in that hospital chair and cried in a way that surprised her. It wasn't tears of heartache. It wasn't tears of shame. It was tears of pure happiness. She took Mrs. Mayhew's hand, which she could not release, and held it to her chest. "You'll never believe it," she tried with a smile, "but Reverend Bower led me to Christ. You were right all these years; I didn't know what I was missing. Now, here's the thing. I'm gonna need you to wake up because I'm gonna need someone to help me with all of this. You're the strongest woman I know, and you can't give up now. Please, you can't leave me. Please, God, don't let her leave me".

She bowed her head as she still clung to Mrs. Mayhew's hand. She just kept praying *heal her, God* over and over in her mind. Suddenly, a weak voice made her heart stop. "If I had known...this was...all it took...for you to...get saved...I would have...had a heart attack...years ago..."

Stella Mae's head immediately flew up to see Mrs. Mayhew's smiling face behind the oxygen mask. She began sobbing even harder as she threw her arms around her frail body. Mrs. Mayhew let out a warm-hearted laugh as she used every ounce of her strength to hug Stella Mae back. She took Stella Mae's face in her hands and again tried to summon the strength to speak. "You look different," she softly spoke as she used the back of her hand to stroke Stella Mae's face. Stella Mae became worried and gently touched her hands to her face. Mrs. Mayhew gave another warm laugh.

Tears began to slip from her eyes as she warmly spoke, "you look like a child of God."

After a week had passed, Mrs. Mayhew was finally able to go home. Stella Mae wheeled her out to the car and helped her into the passenger seat. Once they made it home, she helped her into bed and made sure that she had everything that she would need. Stella Mae gave her her medicine and left the room so she could rest. Mrs. Mayhew couldn't help but smile. She was amazed at the difference in Stella Mae's countenance. Since she had accepted Christ, she was the happiest she had ever been. Her servant's heart began to radiate from her. She came by the hospital every day and would pray with her after reading her passages from her father's Bible. Every time she spoke of Christ or read His Word, her face was positively aglow.

After a couple of hours, Stella Mae returned with a bowl of soup and a grilled cheese. She gave Mrs. Mayhew her other pills she needed and made sure that she would be comfortable until she returned. "Bella is in Nathaniel's room, and she will be here while I'm gone," she informed Mrs. Mayhew, "The church is having a rummage sale, and I told Reverend Bower that I would come by this afternoon and help sort clothes." Mrs. Mayhew smiled and told Stella Mae how proud she was of her. She thanked her and told her she would be back soon. She went into Nathaniel's room to kiss him goodbye and tell Bella should be back around 7:00. Bella assured her that she had everything under control while she was away.

By the time Stella Mae arrived at the church, the sanctuary was completely full of box after box of clothing, household items, and practically everything under the sun. She found Reverend Bower and asked him how she could help. He led her over to a young man who looked to be about her age. He was fairly tall and lean with piercing blue eyes. His brown hair was buzzed like a soldier's and matched his physique. "Stella Mae," Reverend Bower introduced, "this is Chase Sawyer. I'd like you guys to go through and separate these boxes if you don't mind."

Chase reached out and shook Stella Mae's hand. "Pleasure to meet you, ma'am," his deep voice spoke with a hint of warmth. Stella Mae replied with the same sentiment as Reverend Bower told them goodbye and let them know there were refreshments in the fellowship hall. "So, do you live around here," he asked her as he tossed a pair of pants in the box beside him.

She picked up some shirts and started sorting them as she responded, "I live down on Mabry Avenue with Mrs. Mayhew. Do you know her?"

Chase gave a slight laugh. "Everybody knows Mrs. Mayhew. She used to watch me when I was younger while my mom was at work. My dad was overseas a lot when I was a kid. He died when I was six in the line of duty."

"I'm so sorry for your loss. Mrs. Mayhew is the greatest. She took me in when I had no place left to go. If it weren't for her, my son and I would have been living on the streets."

"You have a son?" Stella Mae stopped, along with her heart. Panic spread through every vein in her body. "What's his name?"

She tried to resume sorting the clothing like nothing had happened. "Nathaniel. He's three now. I named him after my father. He died in the war too when I was four. My son nearly died too. He came down with a terrible virus. I, I made some tough decisions, but I am trying to do the best I can to give my son the life he deserves."

"I admire that," Chase replied with a smile that gave her butterflies, "you'll have to introduce me to him on Sunday. I'd like to meet the little guy." She couldn't put her finger on what it was about him, but the rest of the time as they made idle chit-chat as they separated the clothing, her stomach wouldn't stop fluttering. When they took a break and went to grab a coffee and some cookies, their hands briefly touched, and it made her heart skip a beat.

Time finally rolled around for them to call it a day and head home. Stella Mae's house was only down the road about two blocks. She had walked there that afternoon to feel the warmth of the sunshine on her face. It was a positively beautiful summer day. The sunset painted a beautiful backdrop of red and orange over the horizon as they stepped out into the night air. Stella Mae told Chase goodnight, but he insisted on walking her home. "It's starting to get dark. I just want to make sure that you get home okay," he told her as he took off his jacket and put it around her shoulders as he noticed her body give a slight shudder.

She thanked him, and the two walked down the sidewalk as they made small talk. She told him about how when Mrs. Mayhew nearly died, that brought her to Christ. She told him about how her mother practically hated her and left her alone with her siblings and about what an evil man her step-father was. "Sounds like you've been through a lot," he spoke sincerely.

"It definitely has been no walk in the park," she half-giggled. "What about you," she asked genuinely.

"Well, when my dad died it was just my mom and me. She struggled to pay rent. The military only helped us out so much. When I was old enough, I found some odd jobs helping ladies with their grocery bags and mowing lawns. I determined that I was the man of the house now and that I had to take care of my mom," he let out a chuckle as he slid his hands down in the pockets of his faded jeans. "I grew up hearing stories about my dad and about all he did in the war. I wanted to feel close to him, so I enlisted."

"You're in the army," she asked, yet already suspected.

"Private Chase Sawyer at your service ma'am," he laughed as he gave her a salute. "I felt like I needed to do this for myself. To be closer with my dad. After my four years, who knows if I'll stay. I remember how hard it was on my mom with dad being gone all the time and her not knowing if he was alive. I want to serve my country, but I also want a big family. I don't know if I want to put my wife through that."

Stella Mae looked over at Chase and could see the genuine pain in his eyes. Most guys their age that she knew were more concerned about having a good time. Chase, on the other hand, he was concerned about life down the road, not just the now. "Thankfully, my mom took me to church every week. I got saved when I was ten years old, and then I rededicated my life to Christ when I enlisted last year. I wouldn't be here today without the love of Christ, kind of like you said, Stella Mae. God got me through times in my life where I didn't know if I would make it. I owe everything to Him."

The two of them continued to walk down the street talking about their love of God and how Stella Mae recently accepted Christ until they reached Stella Mae's house. They stood at her front gate for another hour and a half before Bella spotted her outside and went out to make sure she was okay. "I'm fine. I'll be in in a minute," she called to Bella. "Sorry about that. It's past Nathaniel's bedtime. I should really get inside. Thanks for walking me home. I'll see you on Sunday."

As she turned to walk in the house, Chase called out, "Stella Mae, wait." She stopped halfway down the sidewalk to the house and turned around. "I had a really great time talking to you," he smiled nervously, "do you think maybe we could talk again sometime over dinner or coffee?"

Stella Mae smiled as she handed him back his jacket that she had forgotten she still had on. "I'd like that," she smiled back as her heart once again skipped a beat as their hands touched. She lifted up on her tiptoes and kissed him lightly on the cheek. "See you around, Chase." As she made her way down the sidewalk and up the steps, she smiled to herself as she heard an ever so soft *yes* exclaimed behind her.

She managed to make it inside and closed the door behind her. She stood there with her back pressed to the door as she was giddy with excitement. Bella came out of the kitchen and asked her who the cutie was. "His name is Chase. He's the sweetest. We talked all night long, and he asked me out for dinner or coffee." The two squealed with happiness, and Stella Mae promised to tell her all about it later. She made her way up to Nathaniel's room to read him his Bible story for the night and to tuck him into bed. She watched him as he slept and laid beside him in bed for a little while. She gently combed his hair back from his face. She wanted what was best for her son and would do anything for him. She would move heaven and earth if she could. She closed her eyes and prayed as she snuggled herself in beside her son. *Dear Lord, help me to be the mother Nathaniel deserves. Help me to raise him to love You with all of his heart and soul. Help me to set a good example for him and to provide for him. Lord, I ask that you direct me in the path in which you want me to go. Help me to discern your will, God, not mine. I pray that you put the people in my life that need to be in it and help me to live a life that is pleasing and glorifying to you. Let your will be done in each of these requests, Lord. In the precious name of Jesus I pray. I love you, Lord. Amen.*

She fell asleep that night with her little love in her arms, the love of Jesus in her heart, and thoughts of Chase running through her mind. And it was the best night's sleep she had had in a very, very long time.

CHAPTER TWENTY

At church on Sunday, Stella Mae introduced Nathaniel to Chase and they immediately hit it off. Nathaniel wanted to sit beside Chase throughout the entire service and kept wanting him to play with him once the service was over. It warmed Stella Mae's heart to see the way those two connected. It was the kind of life she always wished she could have given Nathaniel. She knew he needed more than a mother, but Henry took that opportunity from Nathaniel the day he turned her away. She wondered what Henry was doing now? Did he ever think about the child he gave up? Did he ever think about Stella Mae and did he feel sorry for the way that he treated her? She shook those thoughts from her mind, the way Henry had shaken her and her unborn child from his. Now, all she could focus on was how happy she felt watching her son laugh and play with a man that made her heart skip a beat.

That day was made even more special by Bella's decision to accept Christ. She had watched the lives of the people around her and became humbled by the way she was accepted by the community, especially with her background. She never thought anyone could care about her the way these people had. They showed her a kindness and love that she never felt she deserved. Stella Mae and Bella decided to go out for lunch to celebrate and, reluctantly and nervously, invited Chase to join them. They sat around the table at Weston's Diner as they laughed and shared about their love of Christ and how He had done such a work in their lives.

"I have to be honest," Bella began, "it was really hard for me to make that decision today. After how I spent so many years of my life living in such terrible sin, I really didn't feel like I deserved God's love or anyone's love for that matter. But, after hearing Reverend Bower today talk about how Mary Magdalene was saved and how everyone had God's forgiveness, I decided it's time to stop hating the person I was and love the person I've become. That starts with me accepting the One who loves me." Her voice trembled and tears escaped the eyes of all at the table, even Chase.

They finished their ice cream sundaes and decided to go spend the sunny afternoon in the park. They spent several hours playing on the playground with Nathaniel and playing tag in the open field. Eventually, Nathaniel started to get tired, so Bella offered to take him home and put him down for a nap. Stella Mae said that she would take him home, but Bella gave her a coy smile and a wink as she again told her that she would take him and put him down. Stella Mae's face immediately turned a thousand shades of red as she realized that she was left alone with Chase.

"Wanna go grab some coffee," Chase asked shyly as Stella Mae agreed. He nervously slid his hands down in his pockets as they made their way to Cafe Grounds. He told Stella Mae to order her coffee, and then he ordered his. They sat down in a corner booth and nervously sipped their coffee.

Stella Mae finally spoke. "So, what's it like being in the army?" She was desperate for anything to break the awkward silence.

"Exhilarating," Chase began as he tilted his coffee cup back and forth on its bottom. "You know, I joined to feel closer to my dad, but it has brought me closer to more than that. It's brought me closer to my country, my fellow brothers and sisters in arms, but most importantly, God. When you're out there on the frontlines being shot at and you don't know if you'll make it out alive, believing that God will bring you through is the best defense there is. I'm proud to have served my country, but I've always wanted a family. My dad was one of eight siblings, and my mom is one of six. I've always loved the idea of having a big family, and that's what I want. I want to be the kind of dad my father was to me and the kind of husband he was to my mom. I just, I don't want to make my life all about the army."

Stella Mae smiled and took another sip of her coffee. "I get it," she softly and warmly spoke, "Honestly, I'm still trying to pick up all the pieces of my life I've managed to destroy over the past couple of years. One thing I've always loved is reading and books. I've thought about pursuing a career as a teacher or a writer, but I need to do what is best for Nathaniel. I just want to give him the best life I can. After all, he's been through, he deserves that."

Chase took a long sip of his coffee as he nodded his head at Stella Mae's words. He was doing all he could to muster up the courage to ask the question he had on his mind since he first found out Stella Mae had a son. "If you don't mind my asking," he began as he gave a slight cough, "what about Nathaniel's father. I mean, are you two together or... I just ask because I haven't seen anyone with you around town except for Mrs. Mayhew and Bella."

Stella Mae shook her head. "Nathaniel's dad isn't in the picture. When I told him I was pregnant, he said he didn't want anything to do with the baby." Chase's face was covered in shock. "It's okay," Stella Mae replied after noticing the look on his face, "I made a mistake and some choices I shouldn't have. What I don't regret is my son. Nathaniel is the best thing that has ever happened to me. Do I wish that his birth would have had better circumstances? Absolutely. But I don't regret having him for a minute. In a way, he helped save me from a life that would have only been filled with misery."

Chase straightened up in his chair. "What do you mean," he asked with sincerity and concern. Stella Mae went on to tell him about the neglect she faced as a child and how she lived in fear of her step-father. She told him about how she had too much to drink and then found out at sixteen she was going to be a mother. She told him about how her former teacher had helped her run away from home and how she ended up with Mrs. Mayhew. She told him about how she nearly lost Nathaniel and how she ultimately lost her way, but how God brought her back. He couldn't help but feel admiration at the strength Stella Mae had to have through all that. It couldn't have been easy going through all of that. He leaned forward and gently took her hand in his. "I'm so sorry for what you had to go through," he softly spoke without ever breaking eye contact.

Stella Mae smiled a nervous smile as her heart skipped a beat at his touch. His hands revealed so much about him. Calluses from hard labor. Cuts from the being out in the field during drills. Ink stains where he had written in his Bible and smudged the ink. His hands made her feel safe. It was a feeling that couldn't exactly be contained by words. "Thanks," she replied, "but it's made me into who I am today, and it's led me to some pretty incredible people I am so blessed to have in my life." She gave him a flirty smile and could feel the blood rush to her cheeks.

"Well, I'm happy that all that led you to here," he smiled with a coy smile that wouldn't leave his face. They continued to sit there talking for two hours about their fathers and the memories they had of them. About their favorite things to do and favorite foods. They talked about everything under the sun. They could have talked all-night until Stella Mae noticed the time.

"Oh my," she exclaimed, "I've got to get home. Bella has to work tonight, and Mrs. Mayhew is still gaining her strength back. I'm so sorry. I've had a lovely time." She scrambled to drink her last drop of coffee.

"Please, let me walk you home," Chase offered as he too drank his last drop of coffee. Stella Mae agreed and headed to the door. Chase quickly sped in front of her to hold the door as she stepped out in the summer air. They walked down the sidewalk and picked up laughing and telling stories. She wasn't really sure when it happened, but somewhere during the walk, Chase's hand had entangled with hers. Everything felt so comfortable when she was around them. So natural, like it was meant to be. They walked hand in hand down the street the ten-minute walk it took to her house. They stood at the gate going down the front walk.

"Thank you for walking me home. I had a really lovely time today," she smiled.

"I did too. Maybe next time we can try dinner?"

Stella Mae gave him a warm smile. She walked over to him and raised up on her tiptoes as she lightly took his face in her hands and kissed him. The world seemed to stop for both of them. It was as if all time and things of the world had melted away. As she pulled away, she gave him a smile as she bit her lower lip. "I'd like that," she replied as she turned and opened the gate before heading down the front walk. As she made her way closer to the house, she noticed the sudden movement of a curtain. She couldn't help but smile. She simply couldn't stop. She made her way inside and closed the door behind her. She went into the living room and flopped down on the couch giddy as a little school girl.

Maybe a happily ever after is possible after all she said as she let out a silent squeal as she threw her head back with her eyes closed. With her eyes closed, she could see only one thing....her future. A future with Chase.

CHAPTER TWENTY-ONE

"Okay, you have to give me all the details," Bella exclaimed as she plopped down on the couch beside Stella Mae. Mrs. Mayhew slowly made her way into the room and sat down in one of the chairs with a huge smile on her face.

Stella Mae could feel the blood rushing to her face, but she couldn't stop smiling. "What do you mean," Stella Mae tried her best to sound innocent.

"You know what I mean."

Stella Mae giggled nervously. "There's nothing to tell."

"Nothing to tell my foot," Mrs. Mayhew smiled.

Stella Mae was taken back by her response. "He's a really nice guy," she began, "he makes me laugh, and he's so sweet. I don't know. I know I've only known him a short amount of time, but it feels like I've known him my whole life."

"Chase is a very precious young man," Mrs. Mayhew replied with a smile, "I've known him since he was a kid. He comes over every winter and shovels my driveway and sidewalk. His mother is a member of our quilting club and a very dear woman to me. They're a wonderful family."

"I really, really like him. I don't want to be too optimistic, but I can really see a future with him. I know, that's crazy to think when we've really only been on one 'date,' and we've only known each other for a few months, but I really feel this connection with him. Plus, Bella, you saw the way that he was with Nathaniel. How could I not have feelings for someone after that?"

96

"You deserve to be happy, Stella Mae," Mrs. Mayhew smiled warmly as she took her hand and gave it a squeeze, "after everything that you've been through, you deserve happiness and to have someone there to support you."

"I have you guys," she replied with a smile as she took Bella's hand and gave them both a squeeze. "I wouldn't be where I am today without the two of you. Bella, you've been like a sister to me. I would be dead right now if you hadn't rushed me to the hospital. And, Mrs. Mayhew," tears began to silently slide down her cheeks as she choked on her words. She finally managed to find her words, "You have been the mother I always dreamed of. If it wasn't for you giving me a place to stay and if it wasn't for Katherine helping me leave, who knows what would have happened. You delivered my son, and you have set such an example for me of strength and Godliness. I owe everything to you."

Mrs. Mayhew hushed her as she pulled her into a hug. "Sweetie, I think we are to the point where you can call me Abigail. You've always had that inside of you. You just needed someone to help you see that. I am so proud of the young woman that you have become, and I can't wait to see all of the great things that you're going to do."

They sat there holding one another as the tears came. As she sat there watching them, Bella couldn't contain her tears either. She was happy for Stella Mae and wished the best for her. With all of the tears, she wanted to lighten the mood. "Well, now that I've cried every last bit of my makeup off, I guess I should probably get to work."

Stella Mae rose up to wrap her in a hug. She released her and gave her a warm smile, "See you after work, sis."

"Back at ya," she replied with a teary smile. There were so many changes that were to come their way and Stella Mae's new relationship with God, Chase, and her family was only the beginning.

Stella Mae began cooking dinner while Nathaniel sat the table coloring. Mrs. Mayhew slowly made her way into the kitchen and sat down in one of the empty chairs. "You should be resting," Stella Mae spoke with worry.

"I'm fine," she replied. "Listen, Stella Mae, we need to talk. First of all, I really appreciate everything that you've been doing to help me since my heart attack. It means the world to me, but I can't keep having you take care of me. I think we need to find someone who can come help out for a few hours..."

"I can take care of you. I don't mind."

"I know you don't, dear. But Nathaniel is getting older and getting to be more of a handful. You have this great opportunity to explore this relationship with a wonderful man. I just think that by bringing someone else in, it's going to help eliminate some of the stress that you've been under."

Stella Mae's heart sank. After everything that Abigail had done for her, the least she could do was take care of her. "I'll do whatever you ask, but I really don't mind taking care of you. Honestly."

"I've already been looking at a couple of candidates. They have great skills and great references. I truly think this is for the best." She noticed the look on Stella Mae's face and got up from her chair to wrap her arms around her. "Thank you for taking such good care of me. Now, you need to take care of yourself."

Stella Mae didn't want to let her go. After all that they had been through together, she didn't know what she would do without her. She wanted to obey her wishes. After Abigail had sat down to eat her supper and she managed to get Nathaniel settled, she excused herself to make a phone call. "Chase? It's Stella Mae. I was

98

wondering if maybe you wanted to get that dinner tomorrow night? If you're busy, I under-...."

"I'll pick you up at 7:00," he replied with the sound of smile obvious in his voice. She hung up the phone and made her way back into the kitchen with a smile that overtook her entire face. She playfully pushed her peas around the plate as Abigail asked what she was smiling about.

"Do you think you could help me get ready for a date tomorrow night," the light in her eyes danced as she spoke.

Abigail gave her a warm-hearted smile. "I'd be happy to."

CHAPTER TWENTY-TWO

By the time that her twenty-first birthday rolled around, Chase surprised Stella Mae with a canoe ride that led them to a beautifully decorated gazebo covered in twinkling lights and a five-course meal prepared especially for them. They laughed and talked all evening, and then Chase revealed a beautiful birthday cake he had made just for her. On the plate, in chocolate drizzle was written. *I have just one wish that you say yes.* After she read the plate, she looked up at him and realized he was down on one knee with a black velvet box in his hand.

"Stella Mae, would you make me the happiest man in the world and be my wife," he asked with tears in his eyes. The ring sparkled in the moonlight, was square-cut and big enough that she thought surely NASA could see it from space.

She could hardly contain her excitement as she squealed yes and threw her arms around his neck as she kissed him. Tears began to flow from both of them as they finished their meal as a newly engaged couple. Stella Mae was bursting with excitement and happiness. As soon as he drove her home, she blew through the door to show off her beautiful, square-cut engagement ring that had been in his family for generations. Everyone was thrilled for her. Nathaniel ran into her arms and then reached for Chase, whom he always called his best friend. Abigail threw her arms around her and Bella followed suit. Bella's boyfriend, Vince Whitt, came over and shook their hands in congratulations.

They all broke open a bottle of sparkling cider and celebrated together. Stella Mae felt so filled with joy and excitement, yet there was this feeling deep in the pit of her stomach like something was missing. She couldn't quite put her finger on it, but the thought of what could be missing sent shivers down her spine.

That night as she sat on the porch swing covered in a blanket and curled up in Chase's arms, he could notice that she wasn't quite with him. "Hey, come back to me," he spoke softly as he kissed her forehead. "What's going on in that head of yours?"

Stella Mae gave a slight shrug. "I don't know. I mean, don't get me wrong, I can't wait to marry you and start our lives together and for Nathaniel to finally have the father he deserves, but I feel like there is something missing. I've been wracking my brain all-night about what it is and then it hit me."

"What is it?"

"Remember how Reverend Bower preached on Sunday about forgiveness and how we need to release all of that anger and resentment we hold onto?"

"I remember."

Stella Mae gave a heavy sigh as she swung her body to turn and face him. She took his hands in hers as she drew in a deep breath. As she released, her heart began racing a thousand miles a minute before she exploded words, she never thought she would hear herself say.

"I think I need to go see my mom."

The entire drive to her hometown, Stella Mae didn't utter a word. Nathaniel played with his toys in the backseat while Chase drove with one hand on the wheel and the other clutching her hand trying to bring her comfort. She watched as the familiarity sank in. The corner store she would go to after church with her dad on Sundays where he would buy them both an ice cream bar. The tiny church he would take her to that once was a schoolhouse. The park where her parents celebrated her fourth birthday. The cobblestone street where they would always set up the farmer's market on the weekend. Then the one that really made her stomach drop, the turn that would take you to Houston's Creek.

She pointed out the turn for Chase to make and pulled up in front of her old house. Her heart began to race as she looked at the once beautiful little cottage that looked like what you would see in a fairy tale. Now, the shutters were falling off the hinges. Shingles were missing from the roof, and the paint was chipping off as it fell to the overgrown grass and mass of weeds. Then there was the familiar door with the horseshoe brass knocker she had helped her dad put up right before he had to leave for the war.

Chase came up behind her and wrapped his arms around her as he kissed her cheek. "You can do this," he whispered in her ear as he again kissed the same cheek. He reached down and took Nathaniel's hand as he reached for his mother's hand. Her son's gentle touch made her jump. Her nerves were on edge. She finally forced herself to make her way to the door. As she lifted and dropped the knocker, her hands were trembling, and she felt as if she were going to be sick.

A familiar little face looked up at her, covered in dirt. She'd know those eyes anywhere, the eyes of her youngest little sister, Cora. Stella Mae bent down to her level and tried to wipe a spot of dirt from her face. "Hey, Cora," she spoke in a trembling voice trying to fight back the tears," remember me? It's Stella Mae, your big sister." Cora's face lit up as the threw her arms around her sister's legs. Stella Mae picked her up in her arms and held onto her as if life depended on it. She couldn't help it, but tears escaped her eyes. As she sat Cora down, she asked if her mother was home. Cora took her hand and led her into the house.

Thankfully, Stella Mae had taken notice that William's beat up old truck wasn't in the driveway.

She walked into the kitchen and smelled burnt chicken as she saw the blackened pan on the counter. Two five-year-old boys came bursting out of one of the rooms playing with foam swords. She couldn't believe how much Colton and Jack had grown since she left when they were only a year old. "Boys stop all that rough-housing before you break something. You don't want your father to come home and..."

Stella Mae's heart lept in her chest at the sound of her mother's voice. The years she had been away added rasp to her voice, likely from her mother's smoke train she kept between her fingers. Her mother stopped on the last stair as she made eye contact with Stella Mae.

She took a deep gulp and croaked, "hi, mom."

There are no words to describe the look of shock on her mother's face as she nearly fell off the step. "Stella Mae," her voice shook, "wh- what are you doing here?"

Nervously she replied, "I, I had some news. Mom, this is Chase, my fiance. And this," she bent down to pick up Nathaniel, "is my son, your grandson. This is Nathaniel." Stella Mae could feel her legs trembling below her. She thought she would surely have bruises the way her knees were knocking together.

Marsha began to weep as she heard her grandson's tiny voice tell her it was nice to meet her and to hear him call her grandma. She collapsed to the bottom step and buried her face in her hands. Stella Mae quickly sat Nathaniel down and made her way over to her mother. "Mom, it's okay. Look, why don't I put us on some tea and Chase can take the kids out in the backyard to play. You and I can just talk." Marsha nodded her head, and Stella Mae went over to fill up the tea kettle.

She made her way down the hall to the familiar room Blanche and Virgina shared. *They must be nine years old by now*, she thought in the back of her mind. She opened the door and found the two girls reading books and playing with their dolls. "Stella Mae," they screamed as they ran over to their sister and embraced her, "you're back."

Stella Mae closed her eyes to fight the tears. She kissed them both on the cheek and told them that they were going to go play out in the yard with someone special. She led them into the living room and introduced them to Chase and Nathaniel. She gave Chase the rundown of all the names and led them to the backdoor that led into the yard. Colton grabbed a soccer ball, and the girls grabbed their jump ropes as they ran outside, Nathaniel running after them. Chase gave Stella Mae a slight nod of assurance as if to say, *Don't worry. You've got this.*

The whistle of the tea kettle made her jump, but she rushed over to make the tea. She set the mugs down on the coffee table before going over to help her mother up who was still paralyzed with shock. She led her to the beaten-up old chair she spilled juice on as a kid. She could still see the red stain her mother was never able to get out. As her mother sat down, Stella Mae took one of the mugs and placed it in her mother's hands. Then, awkward silence followed. After what seemed like an eternity, Stella Mae broke the silence.

"Mom," she began," I just want to say I'm sorry. I'm sorry for just leaving like that and not saying goodbye. I just, I couldn't stand the thought of my son growing up around someone like William."

"Stella Mae, don't you apologize for leaving this evil place. I was never angry with you for leaving. I envied you. You think I want to be stuck in this house with that wretched man?"

Stella Mae traced her finger around the rim of her mug. "Then why are you still here? You can leave, mom. Just take the kids and leave this place."

"Right," Marsha snorted, "and go where and with what money? Stella Mae, don't you think I would leave this place if I could? I don't want this for my kids, but it's the life we have to have. I'm just thankful that you were able to get out and have a life." She looked sadly down into her mug. "Chase seems like a great guy and Nathaniel is beautiful. Really." She tried her best to choke back tears. "Your father would be very proud."

They both began to let their emotions overtake them. As she wiped the hot tears from her face, she went over and bent down in front of her mother as she took her hands. "Come with us, mom," she whispered, "just pack some bags for you and the kids and get out of here. We can take care of you." Stella Mae was surprised at her own words. She had expected herself to be full of anger and resentment for her mother, yet she found herself pitying her. She had prayed the entire way to town that God would be with her and to shower her in His grace. She prayed He would help her find the words to say, she just never expected that those words would include asking a woman who practically treated her as if she were invisible to come away with her.

Her mother, with trembling hands, brought Stella Mae's hands up to her lips as she gently kissed them. With tears brimming her eyes she replied with a whisper, "Stella Mae, I- I can't. He, he'll find me."

"No, he won't. Mom, we can keep you safe."

"I'm sorry. I, I just can't." Marsha bowed her head in shame as her body convulsed in sobs.

Stella Mae closed her eyes as she laid her head on her mother's knees. *God, lead her to the right choice. Give her the strength to leave.* She stood up and kissed her mother on the forehead. "Goodbye, mom. I'll be praying for you. I really hope you'll change your mind." She walked to the backdoor and called to Chase to tell him it was time to go. She wrapped each of her siblings in a big hug and kissed them all on the cheek as she told them that she hoped she would see them again soon. She buckled Nathaniel in his car seat and then fell into the passenger seat before breaking down in sobs. Chase reached over the console and hugged her as he kissed the side of her forehead.

They drove through town, and Stella Mae told Chase to pull in to the little corner store. She said that she just wanted to get an ice cream to celebrate her dad. Chase unbuckled Nathaniel and helped him out of the car. They walked through the door and to the back of the store where the ice cream case was. As Stella Mae stood there holding Nathaniel so he could see in the case, a familiar face caught her eye. Her heart dropped as she sat Nathaniel down and instinctively stood in front of him as if to protect him. "Henry," her voice cracked.

The blood drained from his face as he made eye contact with Stella Mae. "Stella Mae," he replied with a raspy voice. He took a deep gulp, "what, what are you doing here?"

"I went to see my mom," she replied quickly. She could feel Nathaniel peeping out from behind her and saw Henry's eyes drop to meet his.

"So is this…" Henry began, but Chase cut him off as he stepped in front of Stella Mae.

"The child you abandoned. You bet, buddy," he growled.

"Who are you," Henry grumbled back in return.

"Stella Mae's fiance. Chase. I'm gonna recommend that you turn around right now and just leave."

"Who do you think you are, man? You don't know me, and you don't know what happened back then. This is my town, pal, if anyone needs to leave it's you. She used to be obsessed with me. So finally, I gave in and decided to have a little fun. Don't come in here acting all big and bad and blame me because your girlfriend was a…"

Chase drew his fist back and knocked Henry so hard in the face he fell back into a rack of potato chips. He hit the ground with a hard thud as his nose started pouring blood as it would spatter while he coughed. "Fiance," Chase growled as he picked up Nathaniel and started walking towards the door.

Stella Mae stood there watching Henry writhe on the ground in pain. She grabbed a handful of napkins and stooped down to hand them to him. The expression on his face was one of complete shock. "Thanks," he half-chuckled as his mouth filled with blood. He tried to blot the blood as best as he could with the handful of napkins.

Stella Mae looked at him with a look of sadness and pity. "Did you ever regret it?"

He looked at her in confusion as he nasally replied, "regret what?"

"Giving up knowing your son."

Henry's expression sank as there was also a flicker of coldness in his eyes. He didn't need to give a reply. Stella Mae let out a deep sigh. "Thank you, Henry, for making the right decision. If it hadn't been for you, I never would have found a father for Nathaniel. Sorry about your nose," she then slowly stood up. "Bye, Henry. I'll be praying for you." She walked down the aisle to the door, and a sense of closure washed over her. She finally felt like a huge weight had been lifted off her chest. Maybe Reverend Bower was right about letting go of all that pain and anger.

She made her way out to the car and handed Chase an ice pack she had bought inside as she leaned over and kissed him. "Thank you, but next time, protect me with your words."

Chase smiled and let out a slight chuckle as he put the ice pack to his knuckles. "You got it," he replied as he gripped the wheel with one hand and shifted the car into gear with the other as he pulled out of the parking space. "I'm sorry you didn't get your ice cream," he stated with a hint of sadness in his voice.

She looked in the rearview mirror at her son reading one of his books in the backseat. With a smile on her face, she looked over at Chase. She ran her hand down the back of his neck as tears brimmed her eyes.

"That's okay. I have something even better."

CHAPTER TWENTY-THREE

They returned home and went back to their normal lives, with the exception of the wedding planning. Chase had training drills that kept him busy most mornings and nights, so he hadn't seen Stella Mae since they had gone to see her mom two weeks ago. Bella and Stella Mae worked endlessly on picking out invitations while Abigail helped pick out the flowers. Everything was coming together beautifully and elegantly. Abigail had also finally begun to improve, which was good since things had fallen through with the caretaker, but she still needed someone to stay with her. Just add that to the list of things Stella Mae needed to accomplish that week.

On the night before she was supposed to go dress shopping, the three ladies worked together making dinner, laughing the whole time and making a mess. As Stella Mae mixed the batter together for the fried chicken, she tossed a handful of flour in Bella's face as Bella returned fire. Abigail sat at the table mashing the potatoes and laughing as she watched the two girls destroy the kitchen as they covered every surface with flour. Nathaniel came running over to them as Stella Mae lifted him off the ground and told him to help her out. Nathaniel grabbed a handful of flour and threw it at Bella as he let out a deep belly laugh. They were having such a good time, they almost didn't hear the doorbell. Stella Mae picked up the white dish towel and laughed as she said "I surrender. I surrender." She set Nathaniel down as she laughed down the hallway and to the door.

As she opened the door, still completely covered in flour, her smile quickly faded as her heart dropped. There before her stood a face black and blue. There before her stood a busted lip. There before her stood a woman defeated with nowhere else to go. "Does that offer to help still stand," the voice quivered. Stella Mae immediately wrapped her arms around her and began to weep.

"Of course, mom. Of course, it does."

Stella Mae helped her mom and her siblings get settled in various rooms. Stella Mae gave her mother her room while she bunked with Bella. The twin boys had a "camp out" in Nathaniel's room while the girls all had a slumber party in the living room. Stella Mae took some towels into her mother's room and laid them on the bed. Marsha sat on the side of the bed staring out the window. She looked like she had seen a ghost. Stella Mae walked over and put her hand on her shoulder, which caused her mother to jump.

"Sorry, mom. I just … just wanted to make sure that you have everything you need."

Marsha took Stella Mae's hand and gave it a slight squeeze. "More than everything. Thank you. I'm sorry to put you out like this."

"You're not. It's no problem." Stella Mae sat there contemplating and finally found the courage to ask the question that was on her mind. "Mom, what happened? What made you change your mind?"

Marsha simply shrugged her shoulders. "The same thing that always happens. I didn't meet his expectations. He had been at Piney's drinking one night. How he made it home, I will never know. He came home that night and couldn't find me. Cora had a fever and had been up sick all night, so I gave her medicine and laid with her until she fell asleep. I guess I dozed off and he couldn't find me. I was woken up by the sound of glass shattering. I ran into the living room to see what was the matter and found him tearing the house apart."

Marsha's hands began to tremble as she recalled the events. Tears slowly streamed down her black and blue cheeks. "As soon as he saw me, he stomped over to me and pulled me by my hair demanding to know where I was. I told him I was in Cora's room because she had been sick. He pushed me by the back of the head into the glass coffee table." She turned her trembling hands over in her lap to reveal the cuts on her hands. "Then, he pulled me to my feet by my hair and slammed me against the banister. He began hitting me with his fists and then the next thing I knew, I was being sucker punched in the stomach with a frying pan. He eventually passed out in his chair. I grabbed some bags and threw our stuff in it and got the kids and me out of there."

Stella Mae's heart sank to her stomach at her mother's words. Tears flooded her eyes as she gently held her mother's hand. "I'm so sorry, mom. Stay here as long as you like. You're safe now."

"Why are you doing this," her mother's voice trembled. "The way I treated you? I figured you would never want to see me again. I wouldn't if I were you."

"I love you, mom. I always have. Yes, things were not the best in my childhood. But I've learned a lot since I left home. I learned how to be a mother. I learned how to be strong despite my circumstances. And I learned that forgiveness is key. I've made a lot of mistakes in my life, but God forgave me. If He can forgive me for the things I've done, I need to have that same forgiveness in my heart."

Marsha gave a slight chuckle and an unexpected smile. "You sound like your father."

Stella Mae returned her mother's smile as she stood up and kissed her on the forehead before leaving the room. "And that's the best compliment I could ever have."

The next morning Stella Mae was up early in the kitchen brewing coffee and cooking a massive breakfast feast. The older girls woke up to the smell of bacon frying and offered to lend her a hand. The boys came running down the stairs wanting to help and went to work setting the table for the adults and creating a picnic in the living room for the kids.

Bella came down and poured herself a cup of coffee as she helped squeeze fresh oranges for juice. Abigail made her way to the table as Nathaniel brought her a cup of coffee Bella had poured. Finally, Marsha slowly made her way down the stairs and into the kitchen. Cora bounced over to her and took her by the hand to lead her to the table. Virginia brought her a cup of coffee and kissed her in the cheek before going back to finish stirring the gravy while Blanche put the fruit out into bowls.

"Good morning, mom," Stella Mae smiled as she finished putting the biscuits out on a plate. "How'd you sleep?"

"Fine, thank you. Everything smells so good."

"Your daughter is quite the little chef," Abigail chirped.

A look of shame flashed over Marsha's face. Bella set out the bowl of eggs and sausage links on the table as Stella Mae turned the oven off and brought over the biscuits. She and Bella fixed the children's plates and helped get them settled before setting down at the table. "Shall we say grace," Abigail asked.

Everyone began to join hands. With an uneasy look on her face, Marsha looked as if she had no idea how to act. Suddenly, she felt Abigail's hand take hers as she gave her a warming smile. Stella Mae followed suit and took her mother's hand giving her a reassuring squeeze. Everyone bowed their head as Stella Mae said their blessing. "Dear Heavenly Father, we thank you for this day, Lord, and all the many blessings you have given us. We thank you for your love and forgiveness and for your protection. We thank you that my mom and my siblings are here with us, Lord, and pray that you help to give them strength and courage. We thank you for the fact that you are always with us and for your sacrifice for our sins. We ask that you bless this food to be a nourishment to our bodies and for your love to be a nourishment to our hearts. In the precious Holy name of Jesus, I pray. Amen."

A resounding amen followed her prayer as tears brimmed her mother's eyes. She saw so much of Nathaniel in her daughter. His eyes, his heart for others, and his passion for Jesus. She wanted to believe in something the way he believed in God. But when your husband is taken from you, the man you marry abuses you mentally and physically on a daily basis, and your daughter up and leaves you because you've neglected to see her pain, how can you believe in anything?

"So, what time are we leaving for the dress shop. Didn't you say Gwen was coming over at 11:00 to watch Nathaniel," Abigail asked as she swallowed her mouthful of eggs.

"Dress shop," Marsha asked as she pushed around her fruit on her plate.

Stella Mae had completely forgotten about their plans to look for her wedding dress with her mother coming last night. She couldn't just up and go look for a dress when her mother was going through what she was going through. Plus, something inside of her made her feel uncomfortable. "Oh, I think we should just push that to another weekend. We have plenty of time before the wedding."

"The wedding is six months away," Bella exclaimed as Abigail agreed. "We need to pick out the dresses so we can make alterations in enough time."

Stella Mae cast an uncomfortable glance in her mother's direction as her mother lowered her head in shame. "We can just go another weekend," Stella Mae replied.

"Stella Mae, don't let me being here keep you from looking for a dress. It's fine. I can just stay here with the kids."

"Nonsense," Abigail chimed in, "you can come with us. Gwen, Chase's mother, comes from a big family. She wouldn't mind watching all the kids while we're gone for a few hours. Come with us."

Stella Mae tried to hide the nervous look on her face. "Yeah, mom. Come with us. It'll be fun."

"Are you sure," Marsha asked shyly.

"Absolutely. We'd be happy to have you," she forced as she took a big bite of her biscuit and gravy. She traded glances with Bella, who could tell she was uncomfortable. She wanted to try and fix her relationship with her mother, she prayed and prayed about it, but for some reason the thought of dress shopping with her gave Stella Mae an overwhelming feeling.

Finally, Gwen arrived to keep Nathaniel and was thrilled to have even more kids to hang out with. Chase's mom was an absolute doll. She works down at the children's home in town and has an absolute passion for kids. After her husband died and as Chase got older, she started fostering children. She had at least six children come through her home, and she loved each one as if they were her own. Stella Mae hugged her goodbye and kissed Nathaniel on the forehead.

They managed to make it to the dress shop in town which was owned by Myrtle Nelson, a sweet elderly lady that attended their church. Her granddaughter, Elsie, helped her run the store. They greeted her with open arms and led her to a room full of beautiful gowns. Stella Mae tried on dress after dress, which brought about many ohs and ahs. After being there for an hour and a half, Abigail began getting tired, so Bella offered to take her home.

"We can all go," Stella Mae offered.

"No, no, no. You still haven't found your dress. I'm not going to let the fact that I get easily tired keep you from finding your beautiful dress. It's fine. You'll have your mom here with you," she smiled in Marsha's direction. "You'll be okay. I'll see you when you get home." She gave her hand a gentle squeeze as Stella Mae helped her to her feet and told Bella goodbye.

She turned to face her mother and forced a smile. "Let's finish at looking at dresses, huh," she tried her best to sound chipper. She walked over to one of the racks and started looking. Suddenly, her mom came over and put her hand on her arm.

"Stella Mae, I know you don't really want me here."

"Mom, that's not true."

"It is. I know I haven't been there, and we never had the best relationship, but I really want to fix that. I know it's going to be hard for you to trust me and I just want you to know that I am here. I am here, and I'm sorry for ever making you feel like you weren't wanted or that you weren't loved. I love you, Stella Mae."

Tears began to well up in Stella Mae's eyes. She wanted to trust her mother. She wanted that more than anything. She just kept flashing back in her mind to fighting for her mother's attention. "I love you too, mom. We'll get there," she replied with a forced smile she tried to make as genuine as she could. Her mother returned her smile as she walked over to another rack to look through the dresses.

"What about this one," her mother asked as she held up a gown with a pearl beaded bodice and a lace-like bottom. Stella Mae's eyes lit up as she saw the gown. She took it from her mother's hands as she thanked her and went into the dressing room. As she emerged, her mother gasped.

"What? Does it look that bad," Stella Mae spoke with worry.

Her mother shook her head as a tear slid down her cheek. "Not at all, sweetie. You look absolutely beautiful." Stella Mae made her way to the full-length mirror and stood in awe. She ran her hands along the dress as tears too brimmed her eyes. Her mother came up behind her and put her hands on her shoulders. "You know, when you were about three years old, you found my old wedding dress in the closet. I came into my room to find you trying to wear it. It practically swallowed you. The next day, I went into town and found a white lace dress in your size and brought it home to you. You were so excited that you wore that dress every day for a month." She stood there looking at the beautiful woman her daughter had grown up to be. She couldn't believe everything this girl had been through and how she still had so much strength. "I'm so proud of you Stella Mae. You, you've really built a great life for yourself." Her smile quickly faded to a look of pained sadness.

Stella Mae turned to face her mother. "Thanks, mom. You know, you have a clean slate here too. Actually, mom, I'm speaking at church tomorrow. It would, it would really mean a lot to me to have you there."

Marsha's purse quickened. She had never been the religious type, even when Stella Mae was a kid. She knew she would feel uncomfortable, but at the same time, she wanted to be there for her daughter. "I'd love to be there," she replied with a fake smile.

"Great. I'm happy that you'll be there," Stella Mae replied with a hopeful smile.

Marsha wrapped her daughter in a hug from behind as Stella Mae placed her hands over hers. Maybe honoring Stella Mae's wish would be the first step to repairing her relationship with her daughter. That was what she wanted more than anything. "This is the one, Stella Mae. This is definitely the one."

CHAPTER TWENTY-FOUR

Sunday morning Stella Mae was more nervous than a long-tailed cat in a room full of rocking chairs. She had been practicing what she was going to say for weeks and now to add to her nervousness, her mother was going to be there. Her mother who had never in her life been religious and who was now seeking refuge in Abigail's home. She prayed for God's strength to be with her and for Him to give her the words to say. She prayed that her mother's heart be tendered by the entire service and that her siblings' ears be attentive.

Everyone began to file in the church. Marsha's palms were wet with perspiration. Abigail gave her an assuring squeeze of her hand as they sat down in the pew. Marsha gave her a nervous smile in return. The kids all loved getting dressed up and sat in the pew in front of the adults. Chase and Gwen came in and sat behind them. Nathaniel practically crawled over the pew to hug Chase. He loved him like his own father and Chase loved him as if he were truly his son. The piano began to play, and Nathaniel returned to sit beside his family.

Reverend Bower made his way to the podium to welcome everyone and lead them in the singing of "How Great Thou Art." Once everyone had taken their seats, he began talking about how today was no ordinary Sunday. Today would be a day dedicated to those who had graciously volunteered to give their testimony. Stella Mae was the first to address the congregation.

She made her way to the podium and noticed how badly her hands were trembling and sweating. She tried to wipe them on her dress without anyone noticing. Once the applause had ceased, she began her testimony. "Good morning, everyone. I'm going to be completely honest and say this is the most terrifying thing I've ever done, so bear with me." The congregation has a light-hearted chuckle in response.

Stella Mae took a deep breath and continued. "As many of you know, the past couple of years have been pretty difficult for me. I left home at an early age and had an incredibly gracious woman take me in." She gestured in Abigail's direction, who gave her a warm smile. Marsha picked at her nails as she listened to her daughter speak. "A couple months after being here, I gave birth to my beautiful son, Nathaniel. He is my light and my life. Everything I have ever done has been for him. But, when I thought I was going to lose him, I couldn't handle it. I thought God was punishing me for not attending church like I should. When Nathaniel was a baby, I thought I was doing the Christian thing. I came to church. I prayed. I read my Bible. But there was always something missing. Nothing in my heart felt like it had changed. So, when Nathaniel nearly died, I ran off. I couldn't watch my baby boy die. I fell into drinking and doing drugs. I nearly died of an overdose. I would have if my best friend hadn't saved me. I think in a way, we saved each other." She gave Bella a warm smile, and Bella tried her best to secretly wipe away her tears.

"I woke up in the hospital after nearly dying of an overdose, and there was my son. Abigail had brought him to me and asked me to come home. I'll be honest, I didn't feel like I deserved to go. I didn't deserve to be with my son after I abandoned him. But if you guys haven't met Abigail Mayhew, she can be pretty convincing. I came back with her and my best friend, only for Abigail to nearly die as well. A woman who had treated me like her own child." Stella Mae had to pause for a moment to compose herself. The entire congregation could feel Stella Mae's heart in her words. Even Marsha had tears of shame and heartache streaming down her face.

"I, I thought it was me. I thought that I was poison. Everyone I had ever loved had died or came close to dying. I lost my father when I was only four years old. He died in the war, and it shattered my family. My son nearly died in my arms, and now this woman I cared so much about was on the brink of death. While she was taken to the hospital, I went for a walk and somehow ended up here, in one of those back pews. It was then that Reverend Bower helped me to realize that I needed to forgive myself. If God could die for the sins of someone as sinful as me, I needed to forgive myself and accept God's love for me. Now, here I am before you. I'm not saying that I'm perfect. I'm not saying that I'm ever going to be perfect. I'm saying that I have been redeemed. I'm saying that I spent my whole life thinking I wasn't enough, and when Christ came into my life, I realized I am enough. When I accepted Christ that day, I walked out of those doors, and I felt like I had been reborn. I felt like all the broken pieces of my life that I fought so hard to put together had finally been made whole. Then I met this, this incredible man who loves God more than me and more than himself. I never thought I deserved love and then I found out the kind of love our Heavenly Father has for us. How could I not love with a love like that in Heaven?" She wiped her face with both of her hands and took note that there wasn't a dry eye in that church. "Shew. I'm sorry. I just, I just want to thank you all for your love and support. I promise to pray for you all always, and I just want to say, thank you. Thank you for never giving up on me."

The roar of applause echoed in her ears as she made her way down the stairs and sat down in the pew between her mother and Chase. He took her hand in his and kissed the back of her hand. His hands made her feel safe. All fear melted away. "That was beautiful," her mother whispered in her ear with complete sincerity as she squeezed her other hand.

"Thanks, mom," Stella Mae replied with a surprised tone. She gave Chase a raised eyebrow and a smile. They listened to four other people give their testimonies about what God has done in their lives. One was Vince, Bella's boyfriend, who was going on a Missions Trip to Brazil in a couple of months.

Finally, after the last testimony, Reverend Bower gave an invitation. "With heads bowed and eyes closed, would there be anyone here today who has had something missing? You've heard all of these beautiful testimonies here today. Come. Jesus isn't just that something missing, you're the one missing. Missing out on life with Christ. Would you come today? Come today and let Him take all those pieces that have been shattered for so long. Come, let Him make you whole. Sinner, He's calling you today. It doesn't cost anything. He already gave His life for you. The least you could do is give your heart to Him." The peaceful melody of "Amazing Grace" played are heads were bowed all across the church. People began going up to the altar and bowing down to pray. As the chorus began to play, Marsha recalled how beautifully her husband would sing to Stella Mae every night as a baby. She remembered how much love he had for Christ. How much he wanted Stella Mae to grow up hearing God's word.

She'll never forget the night he proposed. He told her how much he loved her. He told her how much she had helped him get through high school and that everything, from here on out, would be for them and their family. He also told her that he knew she wasn't a believer, but that until his dying breath, he would pray for her. He would never force her to believe. It needed to be something she came to on her own. She remembered right before he deployed, he whispered in Stella Mae's ear to never stop praying for mommy. She hadn't thought anything of it until now. Stella Mae was his breath. His breath lived on. Now, she was praying for her mother. Marsha always felt that feeling Stella Mae spoke of. That feeling of something, someone, missing.

Before she knew it, she slipped out past Abigail and made her way down the aisle. They sat three rows back from the altar, but the walk there felt like an eternity. As she made it to the altar, she collapsed to her knees and began to sob. Her face was hidden in her crossed arms. *Help me, God. Help me,* she cried as she prayed over and over in her head. The next thing she knew two people were putting their hands on her back and embracing her. She opened her eyes and through her tears saw the faces of Abigail and her beautiful daughter, both with tears streaming down their faces. "I want to believe," Marsha whispered, "I want to believe." Abigail prayed with them quietly and opened her Bible as she led Marsha in a prayer to accept Christ as her savior.

Chase came up beside Stella Mae and placed a hand on her back as his mother knelt by her side. Bella kneeled beside Abigail as Vince knelt beside her and took her hand. They all wanted Marsha to know that she wasn't alone. Suddenly, all her children and her grandson came flooding to her. Everyone embraced her. The congregation had heard Stella Mae mention her mother before in various discussions. They prayed for her and her siblings every Sunday. Now, everyone knew who she was. There wasn't a single member of the church left in their seat. Everyone made their way to huddle around Marsha and let her know that she will never again have to be alone.

For the first time, since her husband had died, Marsha felt love. Not just any love, but a love she had never felt before. A love that cannot come from anything on Earth. That love is from a Father in Heaven above. "Thank you, God," she whispered, "thank you for saving me."

Several months had finally passed since Stella Mae's mother, and siblings had moved in. Bella had found herself a small apartment in town and had moved out. Things with her and Vince were getting more and more serious. Stella Mae constantly joked that she would be the next one down the aisle. Since Abigail's caretaker could no longer take care of her, Marsha offered to lend a hand. They would spend every day praying and reading the Bible together. Abigail was like a mentor for her and helped her strengthen her relationship with God. The kids were all enrolled in school and loved their teachers. Stella Mae had also started taking night classes at the local college to pursue her teaching degree. Chase was training harder than ever, and his mother had taken on another foster child.

The day of the wedding had finally arrived. Everything was perfect. The church was decorated beautifully with pale pink tulle draped across the pews, a white runner down the aisle with pearls on the edges, and white peonies all around the sanctuary. It was a beautiful, unseasonably warm day in March with not a cloud in the sky. You couldn't have asked for a more beautiful day for a wedding.

In the back of the church Bella, Abigail, and Marsha were helping Stella Mae with the finishing touches on her gown. They all hugged her and gave her their congratulations. Abigail had given her a blue barrette to wear in her hair, Bella had given her a new pair of earrings that caught the sun with each turn of her head, and Gwen had given her a pearl necklace that had been passed down in her family for five generations. They all hugged her once more and made their way to their respective places. Marsha stood behind her daughter with her hands on her shoulders. "You look beautiful. Absolutely beautiful."

Stella Mae took hold of her mother's hands on her shoulders. "Thank you, mom. Your dress looks beautiful on you too."

Sadness filled her mother's eyes as Stella Mae asked what was wrong. "I'm just, so proud of you, Stella Mae. Everything you've been through and this life you've created for yourself. And, I don't think I've told you enough how beyond thankful I am for you inviting me to church that Sunday. For that, I'll always be grateful." They shared a tear-filled look before hugging one another and holding on so tightly a lightning bolt couldn't part them. "Stella Mae, could could we pray together before the ceremony starts?"

Stella Mae gave her mother a warm smile. "Of course, mom."

"Please," Marsha asked, "allow me." They both bowed their heads as Marsha brought her daughter's cupped hands up to her face. "Dear God, we praise you for this beautiful day and for this beautiful ceremony that's about to take place. I ask that you bless Stella Mae and Chase with years of happiness. Watch over them, Lord, and help them to seek you always. Thank you for my daughter and her beauty that shines inside and out. Without her, Father, I never would have come to know you. Now I know, I will get to see my husband again, and I will be able to spend eternity with my family praising and worshiping your Holy Name. We pray this in the precious Holy name of Jesus. Amen."

Stella Mae looked at her mother in awe. She was amazed at how much she had grown in her spiritual walk the last couple of months and how she made sure to share God's word with her children. Stella Mae thanked her with a tearful hug. Marsha kisses her cheek and pulled out a large box from which she pulled a veil. "This is the veil I wore when I married your father. I hope it brings you happiness like it brought us. Now," she cupped her daughter's face in her hands. "Let's go get you married."

Chase stood at the end of the aisle looking incredibly handsome in his military uniform. As the wedding march began to play and everyone stood to their feet, Chase's breath was taken away by his beautiful bride. Forget the stereotype that men shouldn't cry, Chase let the tears stream down his face. How had he gotten so lucky? By the time Stella Mae made it down the aisle, they were both a blubbering mess.

Reverend Bower began the ceremony by talking about how the Bible says love does not fail and love is an eternal promise. He then informed the congregation that the couple had written their own vows. Chase began his vows first. He pulled a piece of paper out of his jacket pocket and Stella Mae chuckled lightly at his trembling hands. "Stella Mae Clark, I know that we always laugh and say I picked you up at a rummage sale," the crowd all laughed warmly, "but there's no way I could have found you there. They say who can find a more virtuous woman for her price is far beyond rubies. Stella Mae, in my eyes, you are priceless. I have never met anyone like you. You amaze me every day with your strength, your love, and your humility. God led me to you, and I promise you, now that I'm here, there is nothing in this world that will ever separate me from you. I love you, with all of my heart and soul, and I cannot wait to officially be your husband and for us, me, you, and Nathaniel, to start our lives together."

Stella Mae's tears began to pick up pace hearing this incredible man's words. Reverend Bower asked her to give her vows. Bella, her maid-of-honor, took her bouquet and gave her a slip of paper. Her hands trembled just as much as Chase's. He gave her a reassuring smile. "Chase Aaron Sawyer, I never thought I was capable of finding love. I spent most of my life thinking I was damaged goods. Maybe that's why you found me at that rummage sale." She gave a slight laugh as she sniffled. "In the time that I have known you, you have taught me so much more than what it means to love. You taught me how to have strength in the face of danger, you taught me how to forgive, and you taught me how to have a pretty mean right hook. Above all that, you taught me what it means to seek God. I love that God is the most important thing in your life and it makes me love you all the more. I am thrilled that Nathaniel has a man in his life that loves him as much as I do, and I don't think I can wait another second for us to officially be a family. I love you, Chase. With all of my heart and soul, I love you, until my dying breath and even then, I will love you for all of eternity."

Reverend Bower has to clear his throat to keep from succumbing to tears himself. "By the power vested in me by God and the state of Georgia, I now pronounce you Mr. and Mrs. Chase Sawyer. You may kiss the bride."

Chase grabbed Stella Mae and dipped her as he kissed her before all their family and friends. The church erupted with cheers and applause. The reception was absolutely beautiful, and their first dance as a couple moved everyone to tears.

It was an absolutely beautiful day full of love and laughter, love and laughter Stella Mae would need to cling into more than ever in the days to come.

CHAPTER TWENTY-FIVE

In the four months since they were married, Stella Mae and Chase had moved into a house two houses down from Abigail and Marsha. Abigail loved having all those kids running through the house, and she and Marsha had developed a beautiful relationship. Marsha even started teaching a children's Sunday school class at church and would go over her lessons with Abigail during the week.

Stella Mae had also found out they were expecting and would welcome their bundle of joy around Christmas. They could hardly contain their excitement. Chase painted the nursery with yellow walls and hand painted a mural of Noah's Ark above the crib. Nathaniel loved helping with preparations for his little brother or little sister. He couldn't wait to be a big brother.

On the day of the ultrasound when they would find out the gender of the baby, Chase was running late for their appointment. Stella Mae was already changed into her gown and had been examined by the nurse. She wanted to wait until Chase was there to find out the gender. Doctor Morris finally came in and said that they would need to do the exam now or they would have to wait until the next appointment. About that time, Chase came running in out of breath and apologizing for being late. Doctor Morris told him it was no problem and started prepping Stella Mae for the ultrasound.

"Where were you," Stella Mae asked with worry and a hint of anger in her voice.

"Let's talk about this later, please," he answered with exhaustion in his voice.

"I just want to know where you were. Is everything okay?"

"Stella Mae, please."

"Just tell me, Chase."

"I'm deploying, okay. I leave next month," he whispered in exasperation.

"Congratulations," Doctor Morris announced as he was too busy trying to read the ultrasound to hear their conversation, "looks like you're having a baby girl."

Stella Mae stood there on the tarmac as the other families told their loved ones goodbye. Nathaniel refused to let go of Chase's neck. He held Stella Mae for as long as he could. He parted with her only long enough to hug his mother, Abigail, and Marsha goodbye. Bella had left two months ago to go with Vince to Brazil. Chase went back to Stella Mae and kissed her as if his life depended on it. He kept one hand on her face as the other held Nathaniel. "Don't worry, okay? I'll be home soon. I promise you. I love you." He quickly bent down and kissed her stomach.

"I love you, too," she whispered as she kissed him again as she told him to be safe. She had to pry Nathaniel from his arms as he continued to scream and cry for Chase. Marsha had to take him from Stella Mae so he wouldn't kick and hurt the baby. Stella Mae stops there watching the love of her life get on the plane. He turned around and blew her a kiss as he boarded. Gwen came up behind her and put her hands on her shoulders.

"He'll be okay, right," Stella Mae asked as she watched her heart walk away.

"All we can do is pray. I learned that long ago. Just pray that God protects him and that He will bring him home," Gwen responded with pain in her voice.

They stood there until the plane took off into the sky. With tears streaming down her face, Stella Mae took

Nathaniel from her mother. He clung to her with all his might. She turned around and watched as the plane disappeared.

"Bring him home, God," she whispered to herself, "please, just bring him home."

December finally rolled around, and Stella Mae was bursting at the seams to give birth. Her ankles were swollen, and she spent most of her time on the couch or in bed. Thank goodness for her mother who would travel back and forth between Abigail's home and hers to help take care of her and Nathaniel. Luckily, Stella Mae had finished most of her classes she needed to teach, and she would graduate next month. She couldn't wait.

Three weeks before she was supposed to give birth, there was a knock at the door. She opened the door to find a man dressed in military attire. Her heart sank to her chest. "Good evening, ma'am. I'm Sergeant Travis Abrams. Can we have a seat?"

"It's about Chase, isn't it," her voice began to shake.

"Please, ma'am," he gestured toward the couch, and she reluctantly sat down. "I've been in contact with the into your husband is deployed with. It seems that the area they were patrolling came under heavy fire. We have reports of several casualties, and unfortunately, four confirmed fatalities."

Stella Mae held her breath. "What about Chase?"

Sergeant Abrams let out a deep breath. "I'm sorry ma'am. We're uncertain at this time if he is one of the casualties or one of the fatalities. I'm sorry. As soon as we hear more information, I will contact you. I'm sorry I don't have any better information at this time."

Stella Mae thanked him and walked him to the door. She immediately grabbed the phone and called her mother to come over. The entire family showed up, and she told them about the possibility that Chase may not return home. They tried their best to comfort her, but she was inconsolable.

The next couple of weeks Stella Mae fell into a deep depression. She had been staying over at Abigail's as her due date grew closer and closer. On Christmas Eve, Stella Mae woke up screaming and in pain. Marsha came running in as Stella Mae screamed that her water broke. Marsha helped her out of bed and noticed a spot of blood on the sheets. Stella Mae collapsed to the floor. Marsha rushed to her as she screamed for Abigail to call 911. "Stay with me baby, stay with me," she kept repeating until the paramedics came to take her to the hospital. She quickly woke the kids and loaded them in the car as she helped Abigail in the passenger seat. She must have broken about seventeen different traffic laws to make it to the hospital as soon as she could. She hurried the kids out and went into the waiting room. Out of breath, she told the nurses she was there for Stella Mae Sawyer. They told her to have a seat, and someone would update them shortly.

Doctor Morris came out with a grim look on his face. "She's lost about a liter of blood. She started hemorrhaging once we got her here. The baby is fine. She's healthy and strong, but as for Stella Mae, the next couple of days are going to be extremely critical. I'll keep you updated and let you know when you can go in and see her." They all thanked him and held one another as they let the tears flow. A nurse came by thirty minutes later to let them know that they could go see the baby through the nursery window if they would like. They all held hands and went to look through the window. Marsha picked Nathaniel up so he could see his baby sister. She looked beautiful. So tiny and innocent.

Suddenly, taking them all by surprise, a voice from behind them brought back the tears. A voice full of pain and familiarity. Nathaniel screamed as Marsha sat him down. He ran and through his arms around the familiar man's neck. "Now," the voice asked after kissing Nathaniel's head, "where is that little sister of yours?" He walked over and stared through the glass. Tears began to escape down his cut covered cheeks. "Hey there, baby girl," he whispered as he tried to fight back the tears. "Daddy's home."

CHAPTER TWENTY-SIX

She woke up four days later to the sound of machines beeping, and she felt as if she had been hit by a semi-truck. Marsha had been sitting by her bed, and as soon as she saw Stella Mae moving, she flew to her side. She kissed her on the forehead repeatedly as Stella Mae forced herself to smile. She felt incredibly weak. "You gave us quite a scare, little lady."

"Sorry, mom," she smiled as she tried her best to catch her breath in between words, "where, where's the baby?"

"Don't worry, daddy's got her," Chase smiled as he moved into her view. He was holding their beautiful little girl in his arm while the other was in a sling. His face was cut up, but for the most part, he looked unscathed. She burst into tears as he leaned down to kiss her forehead and then to put their little girl in her arms. She held her daughter to her chest and kissed her tiny forehead. Her blue eyes looked up at her with such a light of innocence. Chase smiled down at her and then leaned down to kiss her once more. Abigail and Marsha excused themselves and said that they were going to go pick up the kids from the sitter.

Stella Mae laid there in awe of this beautiful life in her arms. "What happened to you? Sergeant Abrams said that there was an attack and he wasn't sure if you were..."

"I was in the attack. I actually ended up getting shot. The bullet got logged in my shoulder and they had to remove it. The doctor told me that it hit some major nerves in my shoulder, and he doesn't know that I will regain the use of my arm like I will need to continue in combat."

"What does that mean?"

132

"It looks like I'll be staying home for a while," he said with a smile. "I'm sorry that this is the way I have to stay."

She reached up and caressed his face as she kissed him again. "I'm just thankful that God answers prayers." She looked down at her daughter and back at Chase with tears in her eyes, "welcome home, daddy. Welcome home."

It had been about a month since Stella Mae had given birth and she was slowly gaining her strength. She had to stay in the hospital for two weeks to make sure she wasn't at risk of bleeding anymore and even then, she was to stay in bed for a couple more weeks. She didn't let that stop her from walking across the stage to receive her diploma and her teaching certificate. She was so proud to be teaching Kindergarten this coming fall. Her dreams were all coming true.

At the end of the month, once she was a little stronger, she and Chase had decided to dedicate Nathaniel and their beautiful little girl, Hannah Mae, to the Lord. They made a promise in front of the whole church that they would raise their children to love the Lord and that they would raise them in His image. It was a beautiful ceremony with all of their loved ones present. Even Bella and Vince returned from Brazil with a surprise of their own. They had gotten married and were expecting a blessing of their own to be born in the summer. There was so much cause to celebrate.

Chase also had an announcement. The doctors had confirmed that he would not be cleared to return to combat. Now that he was being medically discharged from the Army, he had decided that he wanted to become a pastor. He wanted to share the love of God with others, and he wanted to learn more about his Heavenly Father. Everyone gathered in the fellowship hall and ate cake as they had so very much to celebrate. Abigail took Chase and Stella Mae to the side as she held Hannah in her arms and told them both how proud she was of them and the lives they were leading. "I love you both, and I wish you both all the happiness in the world."

Early that next morning, Marsha got up to go help Abigail out of bed and to give her her medicine. When she opened the door and whispered that it was time for her to wake up, there was no response. She walked over to her and tried to gently nudge her, but her body was cold. She put two fingers to her neck, and her heart sank. The sounds of sirens wailing quickly filled the neighborhood.

Suddenly, Stella Mae's phone rang as the sirens also startled her. Her mother's panicked and grief-stricken voice was on the other line. "Mom, what is it?"

There was a brief moment of silence before her mother could reply. "It's Abigail, sweetie. I, I went in to check on her this morning and I ... she's gone, Stella Mae."

Stella Mae dropped the phone and it hit the floor with a loud bang. She slid down the wall and to the floor. Chase came running down the hallway with the sound of the phone and asked Stella Mae what was wrong. "She's gone, Chase. Abigail. She's gone."

Chase wrapped her in his arms as she sobbed. How could this happen? She knew her health hadn't been the best since her heart attack about a year and a half ago. Still, she never expected Abigail to go. She was her family. She was like another mother to her and now, she was gone. She didn't even get to say goodbye. She didn't get to tell her how much she loved her or how thankful she was for everything she had done for her. All she could do now is sit there in the hallway, wrapped in her husband's arms, and listen to the sounds of the sirens growing louder and louder until they disappeared into the distance, signifying she was truly gone.

CHAPTER TWENTY-SEVEN

The funeral services were beautiful and dignified, much like Abigail. Everyone in the town came out to show their condolences for her passing. Katherine came back to town with her husband and children, Isobel and Cannon. She hugged Stella Mae and apologized for being away so long and out of touch. Stella Mae just told her she was glad she was here now, she just hated it was under these circumstances.

The family all went back to Abigail's house after the funeral and joined together in a meal prepared by the ladies of the church. They all shared their favorite memories of Abigail, shared in shedding tears, and shared one thing about Abigail that they were thankful for.

"I'm thankful that she saw me as more than the monster who neglected her daughter and that she taught me how to seek God in all that I do. We would spend much of the day talking about things we wish had happened and dreams we had. So, I have an announcement to make. In honor of Abigail, I've decided to go back to school to become a nurse. She kept encouraging me and encouraging me to go back, but I kept telling her it just wasn't a good time. I can't think of a better way to honor her than to do this," Marsha smiled as she wiped her eyes with her napkin.

"Abigail helped me with Chase when he was a kid and after my husband died. On nights when I needed to work, she would watch him or one of my foster children. She was a woman with more heart than anyone that I have ever met," Gwen piped up.

They went around the table telling their stories, and finally, it came to Stella Mae. She held Hannah to her chest while she slept. "I, I don't even know what to say. I showed up at Abigail's doorstep, thanks to Katherine, at the age of sixteen. I was pregnant and terrified. At that point, I was a runaway who didn't really understand anything about the Bible. But Abigail, that woman knew the Bible forward and backward. She took me in and treated me like I was her own daughter. When I accepted Christ, she taught me everything she knew about how to pray, how to study God's Word, and how to live a life that would glorify Him. I don't know where I would be today without her. She encouraged me to be strong, she encouraged me to repair my relationship with my mom, and for that, I am extremely thankful. She may be gone, but I think a little piece of her will live on in each and every one of the lives that she touched."

Katherine took hold of Stella Mae's hand and gave it a gentle squeeze. "I just want to echo what Stella Mae said. My mother loved each and every one of you so much. You all were her family. I can't tell you how many conversations I had with her about each one of you. When I was growing up, I was always in awe of how much love my mother had for everyone she came in contact with. She and my father were the two most selfless, God-loving people I have ever seen. They were always spreading the word of God anywhere they went to whomever they came into contact with. My father taught me courage and my mother taught me what true beauty was and how that beauty came from the love of Christ. I am a better human being because of them, and there are no words...no words to describe how thankful I am to have been their daughter and to always be their daughter. There is so much I regret not telling them. I regret not telling them how much I loved them. I regret not telling them enough how thankful I am to be their daughter. I regret taking all those tiny moments for granted and for not fully immersing myself in every moment with them. Now, I have to live with that regret. Everyday. I know it is going to eat me alive, but I also know that they knew I loved them. I just wish I had told them more often and showed them just how much they meant to me. What I wouldn't give for just one more day to wrap my arms around them and just... I know they are together now, no longer suffering, and I know I am going to see them again some day." She raised her glass of sparkling apple cider, "here's to you, mom and dad. I love you and thank you for the little piece of both of you. I will always hold in my heart."

Every eye was dripping wet with tears. Abigail may be gone, but her legacy would live on in the hearts of each life she touched. She had planted and nurtured seeds in the hearts of each person at that table, and over the next couple of years, none of them could fathom exactly what beauty there was to come.

Katherine and her family remained in town for another couple of weeks to settle Abigail's affairs. Marsha and her family had been left the house in Abigail's will, which Katherine told Marsha were well deserved. She loved that house when she was growing up, but she had always wanted to get out of the small-town life. She did want to go through her mother's belongings and asked Stella Mae to come over and help her. They went through boxes and boxes of pictures and letters. Katherine read through the letters and cards her mother had saved and allowed silent tears to escape her eyes. Stella Mae found a small leather journal back behind the bed. She realized that it must have fallen behind the bed.

As she opened it and began to read its contents, it became apparent that it was a prayer journal. She read page after page of prayers for Katherine, Stella Mae, Chase, Marsha, the kids, and the list went on and on. Some of the pages had water stains that Stella Mae could only imagine were tears, scripture was written on pages along with the prayers. This was Abigail's heart and soul on the pages of this book. Katherine found a whole box of journals dating back to before her parents had ever even married. She found prayers from when her father proposed, her mother found out she was pregnant, and when she was born. As she read each word, it was as if her mother was there with her, reading each word in her ear. Stella Mae asked if Katherine would mind if she kept some of the journals and Katherine was more than happy to let her keep them.

That night, Chase laid beside her asleep, but Stella Mae's eyes wouldn't even give the slightest flutter. She got up quietly and checked on Nathaniel and Hannah before going into the living room and once again began reading the journals. One particular entry caught her eye. It was one of her last entries in the journal, but probably her most poignant. "Dear God, I pray that you be with little Hannah and her mother. Be with the whole family, Lord. Stella Mae has grown into such a beautiful woman of God, and that is all by thy hand, Father. Her story is one of redemption, one of faith tested, one of courage sought in you. I thank you for giving her Chase, for showing her what it means to love because you first loved us. I thank you that you saved her mother and that you brought them back together. One of these days, you're going to call me home, Lord, and I just want to make sure that none of them have to travel the road of life alone, Lord. I know that with You, they never will. Be with them, God. Watch over them and protect them. Keep them under your wings and help them to grow and abide in your spirit. Amen."

Stella Mae held that journal to her chest as she closed her eyes and prayed. Suddenly, an idea popped into her head. Before she knew it, she sat down at her old typewriter with a cup of coffee and there she remained until the sun came up as each key left behind a stroke of her heart.

CHAPTER TWENTY-EIGHT

It had been about a year since Abigail had passed. Everyone was another year older. Stella Mae and Chase were twenty-three and Nathaniel had celebrated his fifth birthday just a week ago. Little Hannah was getting closer to celebrating her first birthday and was finally starting to walk. So much had happened in that year. Marsha finished her nursing degree and began working at the hospital. News had also made its way to town that William had died of liver failure a couple of months ago. The kids were all doing exceptionally well in school and in their athletics. Finally, Chase had completed all of his classes and was hired as the assistant pastor at their church.

One Sunday morning, Chase was asked to preach since Reverend Bower woke up that weekend ill. He spent all night Friday and all day Saturday preparing his sermon. He wanted it to be perfect. After the choir sang and took their seats, Chase slowly and nervously made his way to the pulpit. He greeted them all and thanked them for coming out that morning.

"This is my first time getting up in front of people like this, so ya'll bear with me here," the congregation gave him an encouraging laugh. "Reverend Bower has been feeling a bit under the weather and asked that I speak today. I tried and tried to think of what I wanted to speak to you all about, and then I looked up at my desk and saw a picture of me and some buddies, and it hit me. As many of you know, I was deployed a little over a year and a half ago. I can't really tell you much about it, but I can tell you that there are things that I saw that I don't know I will ever be able to get out of my mind. Some sounds constantly ring out in my ears. There were and still are things going on over there that you just cannot imagine."

Chase had to take a moment to compose himself before continuing. "They issue you certain weapons. They teach you how to protect yourself. But there was a weapon I had out there that was the greatest weapon I could ever have. A weapon that wasn't Army issued." He held up his black Bible, "this was my greatest weapon and my best defense. There were moments I didn't know if I'd make it. I prayed every chance I got that God would bring me back home to my wife, to my family, to my unborn child. When I got shot, I remember my last thought was me praying that God let me live. Let me live, God, and I will give my life back to you. I had the best armor out there that I could ever ask for. I had the armor of God. Please, turn with me to Ephesians 6 verses 10-18."

The church was filled with the sounds of pages turning. "God's word says, 'Finally, my brethren, be strong in the Lord, and in the power of his might. Put on the whole armour of God, that ye may be able to stand against the wiles of the devil. For we wrestle not against flesh and blood, but against principalities, against powers, against the rulers of the darkness of this world, against spiritual wickedness in high places. Wherefore take unto you the whole armour of God, that ye may be able to withstand in the evil day, and having done all, to stand. Stand therefore, having your loins girt about with truth, and having on the breastplate of righteousness; And your feet shod with the preparation of the gospel of peace; Above all, taking the shield of faith, wherewith ye shall be able to quench all the fiery darts of the wicked. And take the helmet of salvation, and the sword of the Spirit, which is the word of God: Praying always with all prayer and supplication in the Spirit and watching thereunto with all perseverance and supplication for all saints."

"We all are going to face battles. Some of us will face physical battles, others of us emotional, medical, or spiritual. We are going to be put through the fire, and the devil is going to attack us with everything he has. What we have as Christians is the best line of defense. We have Christ Jesus. We have a God who is with us in the fire. With His protection, we come out unscathed. We have a God who gave His life for the sins of those past, present, and future. This right here, your Bible, this is your greatest weapon and the source of your strength. You may be put through the flames, but God is going to forge you in that fire into His beautiful, handcrafted masterpiece. My question to you today is, who is your general? Do you let life control your battles and let the world lead you into a war of deception? Or, will you let God be your commander? Will you let Him be the one who fights for you on the frontlines and in whom your victory is held. With heads bowed and eyes closed, will you make that decision today? Will you make that choice to join the army of God to allow Him to be your commander? If you've ever accepted Christ, come. Come make that decision today. Open your heart and let Him in." Several people went forward that day and accepted Christ. Stella Mae was so proud of Chase and his beautiful sermon. She went up to him at the end of the service and wrapped her arms around him as she told him how proud she was of him. He wrapped his arms around her and kissed her forehead. "Thank you. I couldn't have done it without you."

Bella and Vince came up and congratulated him on a job well done. Bella had their little girl, Victoria Rose, on her hip. She and Vince had moved into a little house just a street behind Stella Mae, and they would get together every week for coffee and Bible study with some of the other young mothers in the church. Marsha had also started seeing a gentleman by the name of George Euler. She had finally found someone who treated her with respect and who shared her love of the Lord.

Stella Mae stood at the door of the church and looked out at the kids running and playing in the yard. Her twin sisters were playing jump rope with some of the older girls, the boys and Nathaniel were off playing tag, and Cora was going around picking wildflowers. She stood there smiling as she took it all in. Chase came up behind her and put one arm around her waist. "What are you smiling about," he asked quietly in her ear.

She looked at him and smiled. "Just thinking how thankful I am that God is my commander and that this is what my victory looks like." She stood there watching the people she loved most, and she was so thankful that the ultimate battle had been won and that she had been forged from the fire and was a creation of her Heavenly King.

Four years had passed and so much had changed. Bella and Vince opened a halfway house where they would help counsel young women who didn't have a place to go. They helped them find jobs and would help lead them to Christ. They had also given birth to a son, Jebidiah Colt, and had taken in several foster children. They named the halfway house after her little sister, AnnaLee. They called it AnnaLee's Haven. It was a way for her to honor her sister. She had sadly found out that her parents had both died long before she had ever gotten off the streets. She wished she could have done something to help them, but it was too late. Maybe now some good could come from that horrible situation. Gwen was also working at AnnaLee's Haven as a counselor for young children who had suffered terrible trauma.

Marsha was flourishing at the hospital and had remarried George. Together, they raised her children to love the Lord and would go around visiting the patients in the hospital as the Christline team, they called themselves. They would go around and offer devotions and prayers to those in need. She was finally happy in her love life for the first time since Nathaniel had passed away. She went every major holiday and birthday to his grave and would pray and update him on all the major life events. She would always tell him that there were pieces of him in all their family.

Chase had officially become the head pastor at the church and had led many into the fold of Christ. When he wasn't working on his sermons or going out visiting his congregants, he was volunteering at the local Army base to counsel returning soldiers and to offer training advice as he could. He and Stella Mae had given birth to twins, David Aaron and Sarah Abigail, about two years ago. Stella Mae loved her job teaching kindergarten and loved having her own children in her class. She was amazed at how much Nathaniel had grown up and how, at such a young age, he had such a heart and passion for the things of the Lord. Life had not turned out at all how she had thought as a kid who had lost her father and felt as if she lost her mother. She and her mother were now extremely close, and she thanked God every day that He had brought them back together.

One day on the anniversary of Abigail's death, she and Chase took flowers to the cemetery. She would always go and visit any chance that she got. She sat and talked to her tombstone about how they kids were doing in school and how her mother and Bella were doing. Then, she pulled out what looked like a stack of papers from her purse. "So, I found your journals a couple of years ago. Man, you sure had a way with words." She laughed nervously as Chase put a hand on her shoulder. "Anyway, it inspired me. One night I sat reading one of your entries, and I prayed and prayed that God would lead me in the direction that He wanted me. The next thing I knew, I was sitting down at my typewriter writing from sun up until sun down. It's taken me close to five years, but you told God in one of those journals that I had this incredible story, so I wrote it. I wrote a book. It's about a young girl and her journey through life. She loses her way and walks through a lot of darkness, but ultimately, she is redeemed by God. I actually got it published. It comes out in stores next month. I just wanted you to have the first copy. She got up and laid the manuscript in front of her tombstone and laid the flowers beside it. She took two fingers and kissed them as she touched them to the stone and told her goodbye. Chase wrapped his arms around her as they walked down the hill and back to their car.

The wind blew slightly, and the sun began to go down. One ray of sun managed to shine through the clouds as if illuminating Stella Mae's script. All that could be seen were four words written in big black letters. Four letters that perfectly summed up the life of Stella Mae Clark Sawyer.

The Road to Redemption.

Made in the USA
Monee, IL
21 December 2022